**ONYEKA-NWAEME**

WAS IT WORTH IT?

First Published in 2021

# Contents

I dedicate this book to God Almighty for showing me the vision of the book in my dream and for sending his Holy Spirit to lead and guide me while I was writing the book.

To all the people who read this book, I thank you.

Finally, to SIHLE MAHLUTSHANA and ZIMUZO-NWAEME.

# NOTE FROM THE AUTHOR

WAS IT WORTH IT? – Is a fantasy story about the deputy director of the CIA, Ms. Sophia and her team, against a US ex-soldier Bryan, Juliette his wife, his team, Mrs. Harper his mother-in-law and Mr. Viktor, and the battles that happened between both groups. It also asks both Ms. Sophia and her team and Bryan and his team whether all these battles they had were worth it?

Mrs. Sophia's team are some of the United States top government officials, while Bryan's team are two ex-soldiers, one IT guy and one businessman. With the help of his wife Juliette, his mother-in-law, Mrs. Harper, who was a former CIA agent and Mr. Viktor, who was a Russian nuclear arms dealer. For the first time in history, a Russian citizen is teaming up with American citizens to take down their common enemy, Ms. Sophia and her team.

At some point, someone will be thinking or saying how on earth can a Russian citizen agree to team up with American citizens? And how can they put aside their national enmity and agree to work together without the American citizens feeling or acting superior over the

Russian citizen, and won't the Russian citizen feel like he cannot take orders from the Americans and won't he feel that the Americans would betray him at some point?

Well, maybe in real life it may or may not have worked out but in this fantasy story it did work out. Because Bryan gave both Mrs. Harper and Mr. Viktor no choice but to work together to take down their common enemy, Ms. Sophia and her team. Mr. Viktor wants to destroy Ms. Sophia and her team for killing his only son, while Mrs. Harper wants to destroy the CIA for making her a fugitive. The mission that the CIA sent her to in the Ukraine set her up to get her killed. The only reason she came out of hiding was that the CIA were trying to kill only thing she cared about in this world, her only lovely daughter Juliette. Bryan on the other hand wants to expose Ms. Sophia and her team so that he can be reconciled with his friends and clear his and his wife Juliette's names. Did Bryan's team really gets what they wanted or did Ms. Sophia and her team have the upper hand? Well, you are about to find out because things are about to go down.

# INTRODUCTION TO THE CHARACTERS

MS. SOPHIA - at the age of thirteen years old she lost both her parents in a gas station fire that happened right in front of her. She watched and saw how both her parent's bodies burned turned into ashes and a few months later, after her parent's funerals, she was moved into one of the government foster home care because they can't identify any of her relatives. A few years after she moved into foster home care, the CIA was looking for new agents to be recruited. The CIA director gave an order that the newly recruited agents must have no relatives and no backgrounds. And they must be children so they can train them right from a young age and use them for their missions.

And also, one of the reasons the CIA director wants to recruit from orphanages was because when they are sent for missions even if they were captured by their enemies, they won't have any leverage against them. So the CIA agents went out to scout for young people to recruit them as one of the agents. So the foster home care where Ms. Sophia was, was one of the places that the CIA agent's scouted. And one of the CIA agents named Agent Mike was the one that found Ms. Sophia.

So agent Mike looked into Ms. Sophia background and also into her details both at the foster home care and in her studies and he finds out that Ms. Sophia will be the right candidate for the job so he recruits her. So she was recruited into CIA tactics agents because agent mike saw something specials in her. So the CIA trained Ms. Sophia as one of their special weapon that will be used to destroy all their targets. Through the training that the CIA gave her, Ms. Sophia became extremely dangerous that she doesn't need any weapons to finish off any of her targets. All you need to do was to show and point her to the directions of her targets and leave the rest of the job to her.

Ms. Sophia can handle both short and long-ranged sniper shooting. The more Ms. Sophia moved up in the CIA agents ranking, the more dangerous and the more fearless she becomes. Now all her years serving as the CIA agents in the field, she worked her way up all by herself and she became the deputy director of the CIA. She said to herself that now she was the deputy director of the CIA. That is time that she also works her way up again and becomes the main boss so that she won't take any orders from anyone. And it's either she kills the current CIA director and makes it seems like an accident or she will send him to early retirement.

Now all Ms. Sophia needs was to puts together some special teams that we help her to get to that position as the director of the CIA. So Ms. Sophia puts together a team of some dangerous and ambitious men that also wants the same thing that she has been wanted but in different fields. So her team was made up of four dangerous and ambitious men, making her the only female in the team. And these were the men in her team:

Robert: was the principal deputy administrator of the DEA, that wants to become the chief of staff of DEA. This man working as a DEA agent, was known as the sniper serial killer. The only to be safe from this man was that your name or your organization does not show up as one of the people that he was investigating. this man was ready to go to any extent to bring anyone or organization he was investigating down. This man always takes laws into his own hands and he was ready to kill anyone that was standing in his way, whether they are DEA agents or anyone else. He will make sure that all his victim's death looks like an accident. Now he wants to become the chief of staff of the DEA.

Mr. William: a politician and also a businessman, that wants all his businesses and everything owned to be tax-free. This was a man that owned businesses in the 1st, 2nd and 3rd world countries. This man defrauds all his workers by setting up some fake pension accounts for them and as a politician used the money made for the people that he was representing and used it to fund all his luxurious lifestyle and now he wants everything to be owned by him to be tax-free.

Richard: was an IRS agent that wants to become the commissioner of the IRS. This man as the IRS agent was a corrupted and ruthless IRS agent, that set aside an offshore account for himself that he used to fund his luxurious lifestyle through the money he received from the taxation fraudsters and through the side money he received from the people that he made deals with so that the IRS agents won't press any charges against them. And the only way to be safe around this man was that your names do not come up on his ongoing taxes investigations or that you are sure that all your taxes bills are paid up to date. Because if not are up to date, he's going to find it no matter how hard that you tried to forge or fabricate your taxation bills, he was going to find it and press charges against that person or that company. And he also helps his partners - the ones that he had side taxation deals with - to close down their business rival's businesses by pending their businesses on, ongoing taxation fraudsters investigations. And now this was the man that wants to become the commissioner of the IRS.

Charles: was a deputy district attorney that wants to become the district attorney and from becoming DA and later runs for the senate. This man as deputy district attorney was a beast in the courtroom, this man has never lost any cases to anyone before, this man does not know the meaning of fair plays in the courtroom. For he makes sure that he wins any of his cases, he was ready to go any miles to make sure that he wins. he sorts out who needed to be sorted out and he sets up who needed to take the fall for him. The worst part of it was that he sees all this as collateral damage. And now this was the man that wants to run for the DA office and for the senate. Ms. Sophia put together this team and she was the leader and the brain of her team.

BRYAN- growing up as a teenager loves his motherland and he loved to serve his country by becoming a soldier. He joined the US army at the age of fifteen. At the USA army academy, he was always at the top of everything both in all his classes and in the battle training fields. Bryan's speed was unmeasurable and he always invents some new ideas, that they called him an ideology. He can measure the speed of the bullets and the direction that it was coming from. He seems to know any movements that his opponents will make before they move. This guy never missed any of his targets before. In the gun long-range training, he was the only one in his class or in his team that always hits the target on the forehead and its chest. At the age of nineteen, he won his first gold medal. He was a team player and also, he was a born leader, he always looks after his team and his friends.

As a sergeant and then as a captain, he was also on top of his game, he only lost sixteen out of the ninety soldiers he went on the battlefield with, in one of the countries in the middle east. As a colonel, he quit the US army, when he found out that some of the government top high-ranking officials were using him and his teams for their own self-interest. When he realized that these battles were not acts of justice or acts of peace, that they only sent them out to go and eliminate people that were threats to them, all in the name, of doing what they think was best for the country.

Bryan left the USA army's camp as an ex-soldier with the ranking of colonel but he still loved to serve his country and that he still wants payback for all of his wrongdoing through his times at service. So Bryan's only option to serve his country was to help the police department find the most wanted criminals in the country and deliver them to the police department and also take down the corrupted wealthy people in the city and give the money back to the poor people, whilst keeping some for his self and his team. This was the only job that can keep him busy because he cannot live a day without shooting.

Bryan needs to put together a team that will assistants him on his mission. And this is Bryan's team:

George- Bryan and this guy were friends during his times in service. But he's now an ex-soldier because of the tragedy that happened to all his team in the middle east. That they beheaded some and shots some of his team members right in forward of him and he was the only one that they left alive, the reason why they left only him alive while the made him watched right in front of him and slaughter some his team members were still unknown to him. He cannot bear the trauma of what happened in that mission, so he starts using different types of substances to calm himself down and to be able to sleep at night. Since that mission, he has never been able to find himself again so he quit and doesn't want anything to do with the service again.

Kenneth- this guy's skill during his time in the service was as a gateway driver. But he left the service after he lost one of his legs on the battlefield and he doesn't want anybody to feel sorry for him or see him as a liability to the team.

Ronald- the IT guy, the only way to hide any information from this guy was if you had that piece of information deleted from your devices but if not, he will hack into any server no matter how encrypted that serve was, he will hack into that server and get that piece of information that was needed from him. And it was through his wife, Juliette, that Bryan met this IT guy because he and Juliette were friends and it was Juliette that introduced him to Bryan.

Jason- was a forex trader, only if he had focused more like he was focused on his lifestyle, he would have been wealthy by now. He knows everything about forex trading but one thing about him was he invested more of his savings on his lifestyle than his forex trading business.

JULIETTE- was Bryan's wife, she met Bryan two years after Bryan quit the service. Juliette thought that she lost her mother in the mission because her mother was one of the CIA agents who never returned home from the mission that she went on. Juliette wants some answers about what happened to her mother and she and her friend, the IT guy runs some secret investigation which she later finds out, that the CIA has something to do about her mother's death. Since she finds out the cause of her mother's death, she has been looking for ways to get those that were involved in her mother's death so she can take them down. And then she met Bryan in the nightclub and they started dating. A few months later, they got married to each other.

Juliette said to Bryan that the only way that their marriage was going to last any longer was if they don't keep any secrets from each other. so they both shared their secrets. Bryan told her that the mission that she was on, was going to get her killed if any of the CIA agents that were involved in her mother's death found out. And that was the reason why he left the service but the only thing that they can do about it was to form a team and points them out.

MRS. HARPER- was living a double life as a housewife and as a CIA agent formerly known as agent Knox, just to cover all her tracks so no one will suspect her but the only people that knew about her other life was the CIA. Mrs.

harper as a wife and as a mother was lovely and caring. Juliette, her daughter, meant everything to her. But as a CIA agent, she was a special weapon designed by the CIA to eliminate any of their diplomatic enemies. Mrs. Harper does not need to carry any time bombs on her to destroy her targets. All she need was for the CIA to show her, her target or targets. much similar to Ms. Sophia but their difference was that Mrs. Harper had a weak point which was her daughter, Juliette, whereas Ms. Sophia's weak point was still unknown. Only Mrs. Harper can plan any coup and succeed on it.

The way the CIA trained and built her that even due she was captured on her mission, no matter how they tortured her, she would never blow up her covers because she cannot feel any pain. And no matter where she was captured she must surely escape and she can speak eight different types of international languages. On the day of her last mission before she becomes a fugitive. She knew what the CIA was planning to do to her because she knows too much and the CIA was starting to see her, that she will soon or later be one of their biggest threats. So, on that day before she leaves for her mission, she called Juliette and made her promise that she would not tell anyone including her father, what she was about to share with her no matter what happens to her. Juliette was so scared because she thought that her mother had cancer, so she said to her mother, for how long have you been hiding this from me and my father and also how much time that the doctor told her that she was going to live? So Mrs. Harper laughed at Juliette and said to her, I don't know what you are talking about plus I have no cancer.

Juliette was relieved from her stress, so she asks mummy if you don't have any cancer then what was really going on because she sounded like a person that knew that they are going to die. So Mrs. Harper said to Juliette to listen, to what she was about to say to her and to make sure that she kept it to herself because if anyone knew about it, they are going to die for hearing about that information. So Juliette promised her mother that she was not going to tell anyone about it, not even her father. So Mrs Harper told her daughter that she works for the CIA. And that she was about to go on a mission and that if anything happened to her, on her mission that she should promise her that she was going to take very good care of herself and also look after her father. But Juliette was still in shock that for the past twenty-five years that she has been living under the same roof as a CIA agent which was her mother.

Mrs. Harper told Juliette her reasons for keeping it a secret from her and her father. Juliette loved her mother so much, that she would do anything for her mother, so she embraced her mother and said to her, mother I may not understand now why have been keeping this information secret from both father and me but I know that you had good intentions for keeping it secret from us and I also respect and support your decision mother.

And they both made their favourite meals together and Mrs. Harper went on a mission to Ukraine, landing in the city where her diplomatic targets were. She noticed that some of the CIA agents were following her, ever since she landed at the airport and she also knew that these CIA agents were going to kill her after she accomplished her mission in Ukraine. Getting to her diplomatic targets, she told them everything about her mission, that was sent to kill them but she has no intentions of killing them, so they asked her if she had no intentions of killing us, then what are her intentions?

She told them that she wants them to arrange a new life for her and also to make sure that her family was also safe. And in return, she will spare their lives and fake theirs and her own death. So her targets agreed on terms and she planted some bombs and asked them to hand over their personal belongings and five dead bodies including hers. And they should make sure that nobody sees them and also, they should get some face surgery's after it was announced to the public about their sudden tragedy death. So they did as they were told and Mrs. Harper succeed in her mission.

Mrs. HARPER'S CONTACTS – these are the people that update her about what was going on, in Juliette's life when she was still on the run as a fugitive and they are also the ones that inform her all about Ms. Sophia plans.

MR. VIKTOR – was one of the members of Russian mafias, a well-known arms and nuclear dealer, who moved to the states with Igor his only son with their diplomatic passports. Mr. Viktor left Russia because of the wars that were going on between him and his business rivals. The reason why he left Russia and moved to the States with his only son Igor, was for him and Igor to settle in America so that they can regroup and come up with some better plans and then go back to Russia with their new plans and finished off their business rivals.

IGOR – moved to the United States with his father, with the aim of finding shelter but Ms. Sophia and her team tricked and convinced him to join their team so he can build a nuclear bomb for them, so they can altogether use it to avenge for his father's death.

THE DIRECTOR OF THE CIA- this was the man that found Ms. Sophia and the reason why she doesn't recognise him was that she never met him in person and also after he signed her off into the tactical team, he was transferred to another CIA department. His name is Michael but as an agent formerly known as agent Mike but since the day he became the CIA director, everyone has been calling him 'director'. So the night before he retired, he revealed whom he was to Ms. Sophia.

THE DIRECTOR OF THE FBI – the man who cracked the last mission case with the help of Ronald and also the man that brought both Juliette and Jason to the White House.

MADAM PRESIDENT – was the first female president and also was the first transgender female to become a president of the United States of America, in its history.

# 1 - PILOT

It all started when Ms. Sophia was still working as the deputy director of the CIA. The US's most wanted fugitive, which the CIA had been tracking down for the past ten years was now located in Ukraine. But the fugitive made things so hard for the CIA by hiding at the children's foster care home. He knew fully well that the CIA would not send any of their missiles to destroy the place because they will also kill the innocent children there in the process.

So instead of the CIA using their missiles to destroy their target, the CIA director had to send in some foot agents to the scene. Ms. Sophia disagreed with the director by saying that they should send in their missiles to his location and wipe out everything in there off because the target was using the children as bait, for this was their only chance of finishing him off and if they missed this opportunity, that they won't find him again. What if they lost him, what was the director going to say to the Madam President?

But the director of the CIA gave Ms. Sophia an order to stand down. He carried on with his original plan by sending in the foot agents to the foster care home. When the agents failed to capture their target because he managed to escape from the agents. The CIA director said to Ms. Sophia that she was right but he couldn't bear the pains of seeing those innocent children get killed in the process. Ms. Sophia replied, that those children would've been seen as collateral damages and he should not worry about her or the children and that his main worries should be what he was going to brief to Madam President because he promised her that he was going to the delivered the fugitive dead or alive.

He continued by saying that Madam President will understand after he has finished explaining to her the reason why the mission was not accomplished because as the mother of the nation she will understand. But Ms. Sophia saw his decision as an act of weakness.

A month later, a man from Romania was ready to cut some deals with the CIA and give them names of people that were involved in an attack that happened in Paris some few years ago in return, they will put him under witness protection.

But Ms. Sophia knew if she allowed that Romanian to give his full confession to the CIA, he was going to expose her also in the process. She had to get to him before the CIA agents bring him. She cannot kill him on US soil because it will raise some alarms with the Commonwealth nations.

Ms. Sophia planned to find a way and poisoned the director of the CIA, so she became the acting director of the CIA.

As the acting director of the CIA, Ms Sophia told the CIA agents that she was going to be in the CIA safe room. She said that if those people the Romanian was about to reveal can get to the director of the CIA there will be nothing stopping them from getting to her. They should carry on with the original plan and she will be watching from the safe room and telling them what to do.

Ms. Sophia sabotaged the CIA private plane, delaying the agents and buying some time for herself. She was able to travel to Romania ahead of the CIA agents and managed to infiltrate the safe house where the man was staying and injected him with bio-chemicals that kept him alive for a few hours but he would die on his way to the airport.

The CIA agents collected him and put him inside their SUV but he died on the way to the airport. The agents called Ms. Sophia and told her what happened and she replied that they should abort the mission and give him back to his government so that they can bury their citizens. He was no longer any use to them.

A month later, the director of the CIA recovered fully from the poison that Ms. Sophia gave to him. After he returned back to his position and to his office, Ms Sophia briefed him about what happened during his absence and what happened to the Romanian man.

A year after the incident in Romania, the CIA and the DEA had a joint mission., Robert was working as the principal deputy administrator of the DEA when he first met Ms Sophia. During their joint mission, Ms. Sophia and Robert disagreed with the ideas that their superiors suggested that mission, however, was successful. Ms. Sophia said to Robert that she saw what happened in there, it's seemed like both of them had one thing in common

Robert asked her, which was?

Ms. Sophia answered disagreeing with our superiors. They both laughed and Robert asked Ms. Sophia out for drinks.

Ms. Sophia only accepted his offer to see what his intentions were for his job. Which she asked him at the bar, he told her that he wanted to become the chief staff of the DEA.

Ms. Sophia told him that this was not the right place to discuss this kind of issue. She gave him her card so he could call her so they can meet up in a more discreet place and discuss the issue further. They arranged to meet and Ms. Sophia said to him, that she hopes that he knows pretty well what they are about to discuss and the implications it would have if anyone found out what this meeting was all about.

He replied that he knew and he had been looking for ways to accomplish his ambition

She said to him, look no more because she had some solid plans. But for those plans to work, they need a politician, a businessman, an IRS agent with a high ranking and an attorney.

Robert said to her that he knew a politician and a businessman.

How well did you know them?

And he said he'd known them long enough to know that they were going to be the right people for the job but he will give her, their names so she can investigate them by herself.

What about the IRS agent and the attorney?

And he told her that, she should go and verify the names he gave her first and then, they can set up another meeting. But you haven't told me yet what your plans are.

So she said to him that she was going to give him every detail about her plans once she had what she required for the mission.

They arranged another meeting and she told him that he was right about the name and they set up a meeting with Mr. William.

Mr. William told them that whatever they were planning to do that he was going to be part of it, as long as they can get all his businesses to be tax-free.

Ms. Sophia said to him that it can be arranged.

But they still needed an IRS agent and an attorney. Mr. William said that he can arrange an IRS agent for them and he gave a name to them so that they can go and verify it.

So, they set up another meeting with Richard. Richard knew that whatever a CIA agent, a DEA agent together with a businessman and a politician were planning was going to be a big deal.

Richard said to them that as long as he gets a position of the commissioner within the IRS in return, he's in.

Ms. Sophia said to him that, that it can be arranged but they need an attorney for their plans to be worked out.

Richard said he knows a deputy district attorney that might be interested. He gave her the name for her to go and verify.

She verified his name and set up another meeting with Robert, Mr. William, Richard and Charles.

Charles saw the deputy director of the CIA with Robert, Mr. William and Richard in one room and knew immediately that whatever they are planning will be something huge, very dangerous and very serious.

Charles said to them that whatever, that they are planning that his in as long as he gets to become the district attorney and that Mr. William will help him achieve his political ambition – which was to run as Senate after he becomes the DA.

Ms. Sophia agreed and said to him that it can be arranged but only if everyone plays their parts very well in this mission. If anyone wants to change their minds, now was the right time to do so. She knew, however, that if anyone withdrew from the group that she was going to kill the person immediately.

Nobody came forward. They all replied to her that they are all in. She said to them that they need to build a dark site that they will use for the mission. Once the dark site was completed they needed to recruit some well-trained agents all over the world. But firstly, they will need to fake the agents' deaths so in the eyes of the world they were dead, so they can use them for their mission. Furthermore, they are going to make their deaths seem like it was their governments that were the cause of their death.

But they came and saved them by faking their deaths once they found out what their governments were planning to do to them. They must do everything in their power to make sure none of them has any doubts.

And once they are done with recruiting the agents, they are going to train them. Ms Sophia and Robert trained them, to cause chaos all over the world.

With that step completed, the next step was to find some group or any team that can take the falls they can use for a scapegoat. Once all she required for the mission has been completed, the chaos will be on all over the world and they will step in as the saviours to eliminate the bad guys and get what they want in return.

But they can only achieve all of this if everyone plays their parts very well.

The unanswered question for all of them to Ms Sophia was; what was in it for her? And she told them, that what was in for her was to be the director of the CIA.

Bryan, on other hand, after he returned home from the camp, tried to start a new life but it wasn't easy for him. He tried working at a nightclub as a bouncer but was fired after six months for assault on one of their clients. He got another new job, working for a large company as a security guard. Again, he was fired because he fought with the head of security at that company.

Bryan came to realise that normal civilian jobs were not for him. He came up with a plan to start cleaning up the bad guys in his city, delivering them to the police department so they can pay for their crimes. But he cannot do this clean-up job all by himself, so he needs to put together a team to help him. He decides it's time for him to go out for team hunting.

Bryan met up with George but George was a drug addict. Bryan was so stressed for seeing a good American soldier hanging around in the streets as a drug addict. Bryan went home with George and cleaned him up.

George woke early the next morning and instead of finding himself on the street corner, he found himself on the couch. He asked Bryan how he managed to find him and why did he bring him to his place?

Bryan answered him by saying that he couldn't bear to see his friend laying on the street corner in that condition and leave him there.

George was shocked Am I now your friend? But the time you quit the service, we weren't friends. When George was left behind to die all alone on the battlefield.

Bryan apologized to him for leaving him behind in the camp and also for what happened to him and his team in the Middle East.

After hearing Bryan talking about the Middle East, he jumped up from the couch and started fighting with Bryan. They fought for some minutes until Bryan had to surrender to him and said he did not bring him into his house to start fighting with him. Bryan immediately commanded him to stand still like a good soldier of the United States.

George stood still immediately at the order of his colonel.

Later, George started crying and said to Bryan that it hurts so much that he lost all his good friends in that battle. What pains him the most was that the enemies made him watch while they killed all his friends.

Bryan said to him, that nothing he was going to say to him that will bring back all his friends but he needed him to find his old self again and join him on his mission. By doing so he can get his mind off what happened to his friends. Because through this mission they can take down the bad guys and bring them to justice. George immediately acknowledge his colonel and said that he is fully behind him.

George told Bryan about what happened to Kenneth in the line of duty. They both located Kenneth and told him about their mission. Kenneth said to them even though he has one normal leg and one artificial leg, it won't stop him from driving as long as they don't feel sorry for him and treat him like the soldier he was.

They carry on with their mission as a task force determined to clean up the bad guys from the streets and deliver them as a package to the police department. They will take the cut of the payment received from capturing the bad guys, keep some for themselves and give some to local charities.

One night, after they delivered their package, they went to a nightclub to have some drinks and some fun. Three of them were seated at the bar, enjoying their drinks and chilling, when Juliette came up to the bar to get some drinks for herself and her two friends. She saw Bryan and his friends and said to Bryan will you be a gentleman and buy some drinks for the lady standing next to him and for her friends also.

Bryan said to her, that if he was a gentleman, that he was going to buy some drinks for her and her friends but he was not.

Why are you not a gentleman? Juliette asked him and she also asked him, if you are not a gentleman what are you then?

He replied that he was a tough guy and every lady need some tough guys in their lives.

Juliette asked him, what did you know about the ladies and what they want?

Bryan answered back to her that he may not know anything or what ladies want but he surely knows that they must need some tough guys to protect them.

Juliette asked him are you a soldier?

Bryan answered her yes, I was.

Juliette asked him what happened to him but Bryan change the topic and said to her that he and his friends came here to have some drinks and chill and not to talk about what happened during the war.

Juliette apologized to him, that she was only trying to have a conversation with him.

Bryan also apologized to her for lashing out at her.

Juliette said to him, you see, you're also a gentleman and then laughed.

They introduced themselves to each other, but by then Juliette's friends were becoming a bit worried. Why was it taking her so long to get their drinks from the bar?

They came to the bar to find out for themselves what was really going on. When they reached the bar they saw Juliette chatting and laughing with some strangers. Juliette saw her friends and she rushed to them and apologized for taking so long to get their drinks. She introduced her two friends to Bryan and his friends and they all partied and drank together, ending the night at Bryan and his friend's house.

Juliette woke the next morning in Bryan's bed. She tried to sneak out but Bryan caught her on her way out and asked her to spend the rest of the weekend with him.

But she said to him, Mr. tough guy, so you asked every strange girl that sleepover at your place to stay behind, are you the only one that doesn't know what a one-night stand means?

He said to her that he knows what it means and that she was the first girl to sleep over at his place since he returned back from the camp. Juliette was so happy to hear that and she stayed behind and spend the rest of the weekend with him.

Later they started dating and a few months after that they got married to each other. Later they shared their secrets with each other. Juliette introduced her friend to her husband so he can help Bryan track down the bad guys and also keep him updated on the status of their environments.

The IT guy joined Bryan's task force team and then Ronald introduced Jason to him and Bryan's team was completed. Now Bryan has all he needs in his team to take his clear-up mission nationwide. He told his wife about it and she asked him, are you sure that you are ready for the attention that you are about to draw to yourself and to your team?

He said to her, that it has been his ambition ever since he was still a child to serve his country, in any way that he can,

Juliette said to him, well if that's your dream and if that's the case, he has her full supports but he should talk to his team first and see what they are going to say about it.

Bryan told his team about it and his team pledged their supports to him. He said to Jason– since he works on Wall Street – that he's going to need his help in pointing out the corrupt men and women so they can expose them to the public. Also, they should know that no matter what happened, they are brothers and brothers have each other backs.

It came to the attention of the police department nationwide about what they were doing, in the US, some called them heroes while some called them criminals acting as people' heroes. They kept doing what they were doing with no regard as to what the public thought of them.

Meanwhile, Ms. Sophia and her team have finished constructing the dark site and also have finished recruiting and training the agents that they needed for their mission.

Bryan and his team came to her attention, so she arranged a meeting with her colleagues. She said to them that they must do whatever that they have to do to find Bryan and his team, no matter the cost because they are going to be the scapegoat that they need to accomplish their mission. She set some traps for Bryan and his team and she caught them and had them arrested. Instead of taking them to federal custody for questioning, she took them to another building.

She said to Bryan it's time to find out who the people's hero is that has been hiding under the mask.

She removed Bryan mask and ran some ID checks on him to find out who he was, which she did. So she said to Bryan that she does not have any problem with the clean-up jobs they are doing but she was here to make a deal with him and his team.

Bryan asked her what if he refused to accept her deals? What's going to happen to him and his team?

She told him that there was no way a man with his ranking in the US army didn't know what was going to happen to him and his team. Let's get to the point, she said to him, I don't care how you will do it but I need you to talk to your team and convince them to take this deal.

And here is the deal: you and your team will continue doing what you were doing but I am going to arrange some new passports with new identities for and your team, the flights and also fund the cash that you will need for the mission. Anytime I need you and your team to go and do some diplomatic jobs for me, I will inform you. Your team will also take your cuts also.

Bryan returned to his team and told them what Ms. Sophia said to him. Ronald and Jason were crying and saying to him that they are not ready to go to prison.

He called Juliette and apologized for not taking her calls the whole night. He told her what happened and that he doesn't know what to do.

She said to him, any decision that he made that he has her full support. And he also should know that the CIA are extremely dangerous and if he refused to take the deal they might kill them or sentence them for life.

He asked, George and Kenneth what did they think.

They replied that wherever their colonel stands, is where they stand also.

He accepted Ms. Sophia's deal.

Meanwhile, Mr. Viktor and his son moved to the United States because of what was happening in their home country of Russia.

# 2 - THEY MUST PAY

At the security briefing meeting with Madam President in the Situation Room, a discussion was taking place regarding the war that was happening in Russia and the threats Mr. Viktor moving to their nation might cause and whether he's staying in the US will be a threat to their national security.

Madam President said to the boards of directors that are in charge of the US homeland security to look into the matter, to see what his intentions are for coming to America. If it was his own safety then they should allow him to stay but if not, they should send him back to Russia, whether he came with a diplomatic passport or not.

She was not going to let a member of the Russian Mafia and a known arms and nuclear bomb dealer move into her country without her being concerned about it. But if his intentions are good that should allow him to stay in and if the Russians make any attempt on his life in the US it will be an act of war against the Russians.

The director of the CIA briefed Ms. Sophia about the meeting with Madam President. They should watch him carefully to see what his intentions are for coming to America. While they are busy worrying about whether he's a threat or not, Ms. Sophia saw an opportunity for a second plan to come in place. She immediately called for a brief meeting with her team to update them about their next plan.

She said to them, that they are about to enter the second phase of the mission and this one was going to be more diplomatic than the first. She told her team that, this is going to happen since they don't have any problems yet with Bryan and his team. Robert and Richard should make sure that each of the operations they have been sending their own agents to do, was associated with Bryan's team. Videos of them, accounts linking them to their original names and their fingerprints were found in any of those crime scenes.

And once that was been done, they should make sure that Bryan was seen as the head of the operations. And when they are ready to use them, they are going to poison Bryan's food, drinks or whatever so that he can stay behind while his team takes the fall. They are going to make some fake videos and show them to his team, showing how he set them up. And once that has been done they are going to take them into the dark site so that they will help them to locate Bryan when he's on the run. That's for Bryan and his team, but as for the Russians, they are going to use them for the main mission.

They asked her what she meant by the main mission? They thought that Bryan and his team were the main mission.

She said to them it was until the Russians moved to the United States. Instead of them being the heads of their own departments, why not also be the heads of the operations and then also be the ones that control the whole world. These Russians are not just ordinary Russians but nuclear bomb makers. So here is what's going to happen: since Igor was the one making the nuclear bombs, they must do everything in their reach to take him to the dark site. And they are going to have another dark site, but this time, they are not going to build it because it's already been built and its location was at the CIA headquarters.

So Robert asked her how are they going to turn the whole CIA headquarters into a dark site without the CIA agents noticing?

She said in fury that she was the one that called for this meeting, that they should allow her first to introduce her mission and plans to them. Once she was done with her briefing, then they can ask her any question. So she continued with what she was saying and she also said to Robert here is the answer to his question.

Inside the CIA headquarters, there was an underground bunker built there by the former agents after World War II and the only people that knew about it was her and the director of the CIA. Once she becomes the CIA director then no one else will know of it. They need to recruit other sets of people but this time they are going to be the most wanted hackers from all over the world, IT operators and engineers. They will work with Igor to develop software that will be used as a call bomb to eliminate their enemies. Once their target or targets received their call then their cell phone will explode. That will create another software virus that will be used to cause nations missile defence to have systems malfunctions since nations were preparing and saving their missiles for World War III.

And once they are done with Bryan and his team, they are going to move their agents from the dark site to the CIA headquarters so they can serve as their security. But the new recruits will move in immediately to the CIA headquarters together with Igor. And here is the plan to get the Russians. They are going to create some diversions to make it seem like it was his rivals that attacked and killed his son. She and Robert are going to lead the attacks together with their agents because she doesn't want any mistakes.

So to Mr. Viktor. It will seem like his rivals killed his son, while to Igor it will seem like his father's rivals killed his father, so it can convince him to help in their mission as if he's building something to use to kill his father's rivals. And once they launch the software they are going to take him and some Russians to the dark site with some evidence that the Russians are the ones responsible for the cell phone call deaths that have been killing people all over the world. Not only are they killing people but also they are carrying out their operations on US soil.

So that Madam President doesn't have any choice but to go to war with the Russians. After they heard about her plans for their next mission, all were shocked and they said to her who the hell was she?

She answered that I am your worst nightmare. She and her team succeeded in their mission and Igor joined them in developing their cell phone call bomb to avenge his father's death.

Meanwhile, Mr. Viktor was furious and went back to Russia to avenge his son's death. Mr. Viktor in a rage, killed almost half of his rivals to find out which one was responsible for his son's death. Before he killed them, each said the same thing to him: that they were not aware of him and Igor going to America. That it must be one of the American agents that killed Igor and made it seems like it was his rivals that murdered his son.

They can go to war with each other while they will come in as their saviours to bring peace to them. Mr. Viktor will make peace with his rivals – the ones that were still alive and told them that he was going to give them half of his assets only if they join in his mission to America to find out who's responsible for his son's death. For the first time in history, all the disparate Russian mafia groups joined together. They put their difference to one side and joined Mr. Viktor on his mission to America to find the people that were responsible for his son's death and make them pay.

# 3 - IT IS TIME

Mr. Viktor and his crew arrived in America. They had a plan not to start killing anyone because they don't want to bring any attention to themselves that might lead the Americans to go to war with their nation. But they are going to first investigate quietly by themselves to find out who the people are that were responsible for Igor's death - and make them pay.

They succeeded in an ongoing investigation and found out that it was Bryan and his team who were the ones responsible for Igor's death because Bryan and his team are known as the ones that clean up the bad guys from the streets.

Meanwhile, Bryan said to his team that the CIA can't be trusted. He said to Ronald that he should make sure he keeps every piece of data and every detail about the missions that the CIA has been sending them. In that way, when the CIA tries to set them up, they can use it as leverage against them. That they should not allow the CIA to play them against each other so that no matter the outcome of the missions the CIA has been using them for, they should remember that they are brothers and that brothers have each other's back.

Ms. Sophia, on the other hand, said to her team that it was time for what they have been waiting patiently for, for the past ten years to carry out. So they all can achieve what they have been working so hard for. And also so they can move unto their next mission. She said to Robert to make sure that the four cars that were going to be used as evidence against them, have been loaded with cocaine and nuclear bombs. Robert should make sure that they are on live TV when he arrests Bryan's team.

Again, she said to Robert that he should make sure that every American news channel is there broadcasting live when they are driving out from the warehouse. She said to Charles to get ready because he is going to be the leading attorney who was going to handle the case. She sent Bryan the location of the warehouse and texted him, that he's going to drive those four cars out of the warehouse to the second location that she texted him. He should make sure that he and his team do the job because they only have 30 minutes to get in and out before the other agents arrive at the warehouse. Bryan and his team can take their own cut out of whatever was in that car and then leave those cars at the designated.

Meanwhile, the night before the mission, Bryan and his team were booked into a hotel. They managed to poison Bryan's food in the hotel giving him food poisoning. Bryan was sick the whole night and he messaged Jason to come to the hotel.

Jason arrived and saw Bryan being sick. Bryan begged Jason to replace him on the mission. It was a simple mission, all he had to do was drive to a location and then drive out in the car that Bryan was supposed to drive. Drive the car to the second location and when the mission was complete, he can have both his and Bryan's share as Bryan can't take a share in a mission he wasn't a part of.

For the first day, Jason was present on their mission was the day all this happened. His team arrived at that warehouse and they all drove in at speed because of the 30 minutes' time limit they had.

They drove out from the warehouse and were seen by the American agents pointing their guns at them. FBI agents together with the DEA agents opened the doors of the four cars and found kilos of cocaine and a fully loaded nuclear bomb. The arrest of the four of them was shown on live news.

Immediately Juliette called Bryan and told him to turn on the news channel and see what was going on.

Bryan immediately turned the TV on and saw his friends being busted by the federal agents.

Juliette said for him to leave that hotel room immediately because they are going to come to arrest him next. Bryan, still in shock, managed to escape from that hotel, but he did not know that the federal agents were not after him but the Russians. Because the Russians have located him.

So the Russians kidnap Bryan. Bryan's team were on their way to federal custody inside the DEA van.

George and Kenneth said to Ronald and Jason that no matter what happens they should not allow those agents to play them against each other. If Bryan saw what was going on on the TV, he is going to get them all out.

They reached federal custody and were brought in to be interrogated by the FBI and DEA agents. Evidence was brought in against them about the mission that was linked to them. A lot of charges and evidence were brought in against them along with charges for the past four years for both their domestic and international crimes.

Immediately Charles came in to be part of the case to prosecute them both. The two FBI agents that were also investigating their case said to Charles what part does he have to play in this case? Was here to represent them as their attorney or as what?

Charles said that he can't help it and sat back and watched this kind of big case passed to him and also that the cases were happening under his district.

The FBI agents said to him, that he was welcome to join only as an attorney to help them in the case, but he's not allowed to see or talk to the prisoners. They are going to update him about the case and he said that it's fine by him as long as he's in the team.

The two FBI agents interrogated them about Bryan's locations because Bryan was nowhere to be found. Federal agents were waiting outside Bryan's house so they could arrest him when he came back, and both Juliette's phone and the house phone was tapped in case he tried to make any contact with Juliette so they can locate and arrest him.

The FBI agents told Bryan's team that they are going to away for a very long time with the evidence they had against them. They should help them locate Bryan so they can cut a deal with them and limit their time in prison.

But they all said the same thing to those agents – they need their lawyers and to make a phone call which was their legal right.

Both the FBI and DEA agents tried to break them but they did not give in. Two FBI investigating agents said to each other that something seems off about this case. They looked at these guy backgrounds – even Bryan's – and they could not believe what they saw.  Even with all the evidence that they had with them, they couldn't believe that these four guys were the ones that carried all these missions – both domestic and international – by themselves. Either someone was using them or they had been set up.

The two agents planned to run another investigation by themselves. But Robert noticed what was going on.

Immediately he contacted Ms. Sophia and told her that they needed to meet up.

They met up and Robert told her about what he suspected about the FBI agents. Ms. Sophia said to him that the FBI should not be part of his worries for now, that he should focus on the mission and get those guys prosecuted. They will use the two FBI agents as loose ends so that the other FBI agents will focus on arresting Bryan for killing their agents.

Meanwhile, Bryan was with the Russians. The Russians had been torturing him, for information on the reasons why he killed Mr. Viktor's son and where they can find the other people that helped him out in carrying out the mission. But Bryan kept on saying to them that he does not know what they are talking about and that he has never met Mr. Viktor or his son before.

But they kept on torturing him and he kept on saying the same thing.

Mr. Viktor said to him, even though he's not the one that killed his son but since he was aware of what he and his team has been doing, that they are going to find his son's killers for him. So Bryan told him what had happened to his team and Mr. Viktor said: " well, you are now a fugitive so why wouldn't I hand you over to your government, in exchange for them giving me, the names of my son's killers. Bryan replied back to him by saying those are the same people that he is going to hand him over to was the same people that killed his son, so what makes him so sure that they are going to give him what he wants or they are going to kill him as well like they killed his son.

Mr. Viktor in rage hits Bryan over and over again. But one of the mafias said to him that this American was the only chance for them to get the names of his son's killers, so he stops hitting him. Mr Viktor said to Bryan that he is going to give him some of his men to go and find his son's real killers. Since he is the country's most wanted man, that he's going to stay with him until everything settles down a bit that way he could carry on with his mission to find him, his son's real killers since he's not the killer.

Meanwhile, Bryan's friends were in prison awaiting their court hearings. The CIA set in, on the case and took over the case from the FBI and DEA, before the case in particular posed threats to their country's relationship with both the international and Commonwealth countries. The prisoners were moved into CIA custody.

And Ms. Sophia invited the two FBI agents as she needed them to be part of the ongoing investigation. They happily accepted and joined the task force team. The prisoners were transferred to the CIA headquarters and it was all part of Ms. Sophia's plan to move them to the CIA headquarters, as it will much easier for her to get to them.

Ms. Sophia secretly went in where the prisoners were and they are so excited to see her. She said to them that they did a very good job by keeping their mouths closed and that she would get to the bottom of the case to find out who was responsible for setting them up. She explained the plan to the prisoners as it was the only way for them to get out of the mess. She exclaimed that they must do as they are told as if they want to get out of the mess. Ms. Sophia posed a question to them regarding their freedom their response was unanimous they all agreed they wanted to get out, so she went on to explain the plan. The plan proceeded as follows when they get to court tomorrow, they should plead guilty to all charges that level against them in the courtroom. That Bryan was the head of their operations and they took them to a cell before moving them to the federal prison.

She would inject them with some chemicals that will make their heart stop beating for the next 24 hours and that will make it seem as if Bryan killed them for exposing him. Once it was made known to the public they were dead she would take them to a dark site where they will wait

And they all agreed to the plan but the only reason they agreed was to save themselves from going to prison. She left and went straight to the CIA director's office and said to him, that she wants every high ranking prosecutor and attorney to participate in this case, that way it won't seem like the CIA was taking over everything. The director asked her who she had in mind but in response, she stated that she does not have anyone in mind and that the FBI agents involved in the case can give their input on who they think should be the leading prosecutor and attorney to lead the case. The FBI agents referred Charles to them to be the leading prosecutor for the case because they did not want to be biased for this case and that they wanted the prisoners to get some fair traits for this case.

The FBI agents only did that so they could buy themselves more time to investigate what was really going on with the case. Ms. Sophia said to Charles that she had already arranged everything for him with the prisoners, that all he needs to do was to play his part tomorrow in the courtroom. The day of court arrives with Charles as the leading prosecutor and attorney they won the case by making the prisoners plead guilty and by accepting that Bryan was their leader as well as the head of their operation.

Both madam president and the whole of America were thanking all the agents for their endless efforts in bringing justice to their nation. Both the judge and madam president declared Bryan as the most wanted terrorist in their country as well as in the other nations which he carried out all those missions.

The FBI agents did not agree on the judgment that had been passed on. As well as on Bryan because those men gave in so easily. They tried everything in their power to break those four guys but refused to give them any names, let alone even mention Bryan's name initially and now for the four men to plead guilty before the judge and before everyone else just didn't seem right.

Then they agreed that this case was way bigger than they thought it was and that the people behind everything was right in front of them. They needed to investigate and find out for themselves. The prisoners were kept inside the federal cell as they were told and was waiting to be transferred to the federal prison in the morning. Ms. Sophia came in immediately and injected some of the chemicals into their bloodstream and early the next morning the prison wardens came to transfer them to their prison cell as the judge sentenced them to twenty years in prison but there is a possibility they could be released after fifteen years on good behaviour. The reason behind this is because the judge took into consideration that they complied with the law and it was the first time pleading guilty in the court of law.

The wardens found them lying dead in their cells, so they alarmed the whole unit. Every agent came into the cell excluding Ms. Sophia and confirmed their death. Ms. Sophia as the leading agent on the case after they informed her what had just happened to the prisoners, said to them immediately that it was Bryan and that they should think of it, the whole time that the guys refused to give or mention any names to them that they were still alive, why is it now that when they gave Bryan's name to them suddenly they all dead? Ms Sophia stated it was time to pay Bryan's wife a visit and bring her in for questioning.

# 4 - I WANT HIM DEAD OR ALIVE

Meanwhile, Juliette was still devastated to see what was going on as well as why she hasn't heard from Bryan since the day of the incident. She was also in belief as to why Bryans friends would turn against him after everything that he has done for them. Juliette woke up early in the morning to see what was going on in the news, to see whether they had arrested her husband or not but only to find out on the news that Bryan's friends were all dead and it was her husband that was responsible for their deaths.

The news added more anxiety to Juliette, she immediately started packing her bags to leave as she knew that the FBI agents would be coming after her next. To her surprise, she was greeted by their presence as she opened the front door. The agents detained her immediately and said: Ma'am you have the right to remain silent, anything you say right now can and will be used against you in the court of law. You have the right to get an attorney and if you cannot afford one the state will provide you with one.

They arrested her but on the way to the federal custody, the two FBI agents said to her, ma'am we are your side here, we also do not believe all those accusations levelled up against your husband but that she has to help them so that they would be able to help her too. Juliette remained silent.

Upon the arrival of Juliette at the station, Ms. Sophia said to them that they should make it known to the public that the terrorist wife has been arrested, and that she is in their custody right now. They did as they were told and Ms. Sophia said to the agents that they should watch and learn. The reason why she wanted them to make it known to the public was that whenever Bryan was, going to come out of hiding now that he knows that they have his wife in custody. Ms Sophia gave an instruction that should watch where they kept her that nobody should come in or out of the facility that she is. She assigned the two FBI agents to watch her and she also instructed that nobody should talk or make any contact with her and that she was only there as bait to lure Bryan in.

Everyone left, leaving Juliette with the two FBI agents but Ms. Sophia was watching the two FBI agents through the cameras to see what they were going to do, whether they would make any contact with her or not. But those two FBI agents disobeyed her and made contact with Juliette by saying to her, if she knew her husband's location that now was the right time, she should give it to them before the other federal agents could get to him.

Juliette replied that she did not have anything to say to them but, that she wanted her lawyer and a packet of cigarettes to smoke since they had kept her here the whole morning up until now. She needed something to smoke to calm herself down before she went insane in here. They gave her a packet of cigarettes and a lighter, so she used it to light up the cigarettes.

They asked her again if she knew anyone that might do this to her husband or if there were people that were working with her husband in secret. She replied back to them, "I wish I have something to give to you, but I don't. Anyways, thank you guys for the packet of cigarettes." As Ms. Sophia was seeing all of the incidents that were occurring between Juliette and the two agents, she suggested to Robert that he should make sure that when transporting Juliette to another location, that he arranges their own secret agents in convoy with those agents and, once Bryan had arrived to break his wife out, that the two FBI agents had to be killed in order to make it seem as if Bryan was the one that killed them. This way, the FBI and all of their agents would be focused on catching Bryan for killing their two agents.

Meanwhile, Bryan, would be at the place that Mr. Viktor was hiding him and, saw how his friends had betrayed him. He also saw that they were dead and that Ms. Sophia claimed that he was responsible for their deaths. Ms. Sophia had also made it known of the news that they had arrested Juliette, his wife. In a blind rage, he said to Mr. Viktor that he should give him some of his men so that he could go and break his wife out of federal custody and once he got his wife, he vowed to do anything in his power to find and convict his son's real killers.

Mr. Viktor laughed at him and said to him, "you American's" because, he did not understand how American's behave in that Bryan should be the one taking orders from him, not the other way around.

The only reason why he was still alive was that he needed him to find his son's real killers and he said to him, "So you American, tell me, what are you going to do when you get to the federal custody, and how many federal agents do you think you and my men could handle if I gave them to you? How many men are going to die before you even arrive at the place that they kept your wife, Mm-hmm!"

"You tell me?"

He didn't want to involve his men in whatever Bryan was planning to do because, the American's will see it as the Russians helping him out, all the while so that they can go to war with the Russians. He was not going to be the reason why there could be wars between his nation and America.

Bryan kept on pleading to him, to help him out and one of the mafias whispered to him that they should help him out since his wife was so important to him, so by helping him break his wife out, this was going to push him even further to find his son's killers.

Mr. Viktor agreed to help him but said that they were going to use his plan to break his wife out and that he was not ready to send in his men on Bryan's suicide mission. Bryan agreed with him, as long as he was going to get his wife out. Mr. Viktor explained to him what was going to happen, that he was going to send some of his men to watch where they were keeping his wife, and once they confirmed that his wife was about to be transported to another government facility, and his men were going to alert him on how many convoys they were using to transport his wife, so he could know how many men that they were going to travel with. His men would follow them so that they could alert him to the routes that they were travelling on so that they could wait for them along the way and breaks his wife out. Bryan thanked him for his plans and for agreeing to participate in the mission.

Meanwhile, Mrs. Harper saw in the news that her Juliette had been arrested by the federal agents. She had said to herself that there was no way that she was going to allow herself to sit back and watch while the US government took the only thing that was so precious to her away. The only thing that was stopping her from exposing the CIA and their secrets, was the fact that she was forced into hiding for over a decade now and it was all because she knew that they would go after her and kill both her and her father once she exposed them. Now it was the same situation with the CIA, except that they were planning to kill her only daughter.

She said that she cannot allow this to happen, not under her watch. She knew the routes that the federal agents were going to use to transport her daughter, so she went and surveyed those routes because everywhere had changed and had been developed.

So, on the next day that they were transporting Juliette to another location, Ms. Sophia said to all the agents that they were only using Juliette as bait, to smoke out Bryan from his hiding place and, that they should also be on their guard, always be watchful because he may attack them at any moment when they were least expecting him.

Ms. Sophia, together with other government agents, were watching them in a room while they were making their way to the next location. They were driving out from the city, getting onto some remote routes, when Mrs. Harper attacked them and killed all the agents inside the convoy, while she escaped with Juliette her daughter.

While Ms. Sophia and the agents, that were watching with them, were busy trying to call in all units to see whether anyone would respond to their call. The only thing that they saw was the bomb that destroyed the first conveys in lines and the next thing that they saw was the smoke everywhere. Before Bryan, Mr. Viktor and his men got to the location the only things that they saw was first some heavy smoke and the agents that were transporting Juliette laid dead on the floor and his wife was nowhere to be seen. He noticed that they had been hijacked.

Mr. Viktor said to him that they have to leave right now before the other agents approached the scene. They left the scene and Bryan was still devastated about what happened to his wife and if she was still alive. He wondered who might have her in their custody. Bryan turned on the TV to see want was going on on the news. He saw in the news, that madam president was saying that he is responsible for the attacks that happened earlier that day because the whole federal agents briefed her that Bryan was responsible for the attacks. America loss her sons and daughters as well as some for their colleagues and good agents and to the families who lost their sons, daughters, husbands and wives in the attacks.

Madam President gave an executive order that the whole country should be on lockdown, nobody could leave or enter into the country as all the borders were to be closed. Madam President instructed them to put Bryans picture everywhere and that the forces should approach carefully when they find him and if he surrenders himself to them willing that they should arrest him if he shoots at them first that they shouldn't hesitate to shoot him back. She clearly stated she wants him caught! Whether it is dead or alive.

# 5 - BACK TO THE ORIGINAL PLAN

Ms. Sophia called Robert aside and asked him if he wanted to know the real truth about what happened at the scene today. Robert responded with a yes stating that he wanted to know the real truth as he still has doubts that Bryan was behind the attacks that occurred earlier that day. Ms Sophia began explaining exactly what had happened she said to Robert that the reason she carried out this plan and told Madam President that Bryan was the one who carried out those attacks was that she was not sure if her conspiracies were correct and due to the fact that Madam President wanted answers from her she had to quickly come out with a fabrication.

Robert asked her what were her theories? She said that she is still putting them together because for the past four years that she has been sending Bryan on missions. She had seen what Bryan was capable of doing and that he can only do that with help of his team members. And that there was no way that Bryan can put together a team to help him carry out that attack under such short notice.

The only one she knows that was capable of doing so, was agent Knox but what confused her was that agent

Knox dead ten years ago. She was not sure what really happened to agent Knox whilst on her mission in Ukraine whether she was truly dead or not because the CIA made sure that her death was concealed because the only one that could go through her case files was the CIA director. During that time she discovered that Juliette was her daughter and that is either agent Knox carried that attack on her own daughter or that she teamed up with Bryan but whichever one it was, that it was time they go back to their original plan and pay a visit to George, Kenneth, Ronald and Jason at the dark site.

This way they could help them locate Bryan, so she could find out for herself what was really going on. They were the only ones that would make it much easier to locate Bryan than anyone else. Robert asked her how she managed to get George, Kenneth, Ronald and Jason and secure them to the dark site.

She laughed and told him that she managed to secure them to the dark site by carrying out the perfect plan, she goes on to explain and tells Robert how she switched the cars at the memorial service as the cars were about to leave for the cemetery furthermore she went on to add that in the coffins were plastic replicas.

Robert praised her by saying how well she executed the plan and that she is very well prepared for the mission. Robert asked Ms Sophia how they were holding up at the campsite she responded with a smile on her face; pretty well.

Robert asked her what did you mean by pretty well?

She replied to him by saying that she makes sure that there is no way that they could locate the dark site because they would wake up at night and see night as their day while during the day they are asleep that way when they are awake the other agents are asleep and vice versa. She stated that she put some restrictions on them, that they are only allowed to use the game room, the restroom and the kitchens and that she make sure that Ronald is not able to hack any of their serves by putting some limits on his daily data and things that he could research and if he tries anything other than that, that his computer was going show a blue screen and then shuts down immediately and it would remain off for the rest of the day.

Robert asked her, what she was waiting for and that they should start making their way to the dark site. They both laughed and began to make their way to the dark site. They made sure that they got to the dark site in the evening that way the hostages would not notice the difference between day and night.

They met up with Bryan's friends and asked them how they were adapting to their new lives and they all answered that was important to them that they stayed alive and that they are free from prison. They all thanked Ms. Sophia for helping them all out. Ms. Sophia acknowledged their praises to her and said to them that they should wait until she gives to them the name and the person that was responsible for setting them up, just as she promised.

She showed to them the fake video that Bryan made to set them up, they were all furious and said: 'After everything we've done for Bryan this is the way he thanks us '.

George said that he could not wait to find Bryan and kill him with his own hands.

Ms. Sophia said to him that he should not kill Bryan. Ms Sophia told the hostages their new plan and what was going to happen was that she was going to move them to the city that way they could help locate Bryan. She went on to say that once they locate Bryan that they should alert her so that she could arrest Bryan and make him pay for all his crimes.

Behind closed doors, the hostages said that the only reason they pretended to be angry when Ms Sophia showed them the fake video was so that they could be moved into the city from the dark site. Robert asked Ms. Sophia if she thought that they bought the cover-up of the fake video or if they were just pretending? She replied back to him by saying:' whether they believed it or not, it was none of her business and that one thing that she is sure of is that they are going to locate or make contact with Bryan one way or another.'

'She said that she was going to send in two of their agents to follow them and once they locate or makes any contacts with them, that their agents will alert them and also if one makes contact with Bryan their location would be exposed and they would be able to kill them all. The catch, however, what that in order for this plan to be carried out perfectly she needed them to be out of the dark site in order for the original plan to be carried out. On the other hand, the hostages pretend by agreeing to her plan so they can find Bryan and reconcile with him and tell him that the reason they said what they said about him in the courtroom was so that they could all come back with a better plan and finish off Ms. Sophia and her team once and for all. Ms. Sophia injected them and move them to the city and also made a new identity for them. She left some money for them, a phone and all the equipment that they need for that mission. She also left her two agents that would be secretly watching them all the time.

Meanwhile, Bryan on the other hand was still devastated about what could have happened to his wife. Mr. Viktor came up to where he was and asked him how he was holding up but Bryan did not say a word to him. Mr. Viktor said to him that he knows how he was feeling right now and that he felt the same way on the night Igor his son died and that he now believed that Bryan was truly not his sons real killer. Mr Viktor told Bryan that he should not be too hard on himself as not everything always goes as planned. He went on to explain that he came to America with his son to find another way to finish off his business rivals in Russia and now the same rivals are the ones helping him find his son's killers.

As he was about to leave, Bryan asked him, how did your son die? He replied back by saying that one night while his son and himself were sleeping both in separate rooms that gunfire began out of nowhere, and that they were shooting and bombing everywhere at the same time and before he could make his way to his son's room it had been bombed already.

Bryan comforted him about his son's death as well and asked Mr Viktor if he was now fully convinced that he was not his son's real killer?

Bryan asked Mr Viktor if he thought there were any similarities between the kidnapping of his wife and Mr Viktor's son's death?

Mr Viktor responded by saying that they came in and out before anyone could notice anything and the thing that made things even worse, was that he was living thousands of miles away from the city.

Bryan asked Mr Viktor are you thinking what I am thinking?'

Mr. Viktor answered him back "yes". Mr Viktor went on to say this means that if we find the people who kidnapped your wife we will find my sons killers as well. Bryan that since he's the worlds most wanted man he is going to sit back while his contacts in America try to locate the people who kidnapped his wife and once he finds them that he would kill them. Mr Viktor asked Bryan how he was going to clear his name once he finds his wife.

Due to the fact that he knew the agents set him up. He replied back to him by saying that he does not have a plan yet but the only thing that matters right now, was his wife Juliette. Meanwhile, Juliette woke up from the place that her mother kept her and she went down the stairs to find out where she was. At first, her thought was that Bryan was the one who attacked the agents and kidnapped her and brought her to this place for some safekeeping. Only for her to go downstairs and find a table full of all her favourite meals and her mother standing next to the table.

She immediately saw her mother and fainted because she thought that she had just seen her mother's ghost. Her mother woke her up and she fainted again three consecutive times.

Juliette asked who are you?

She answered I'm your mother and Juliette said back to her that her mother had died ten years ago.

But Mrs. Harper said to her that she was still alive. Juliette asked how are you still alive? Mrs. Harper said back to her that she never died in the first place. Juliette said that maybe she was still affected by the attack that happened yesterday that she needed to go get some rest. Juliette went up and tried to escape through the window but her mother caught her just in time and said to her: my daughter you haven't changed a bit.

Little did her mother know that once she went to sleep, Juilette would try and escape again.

This was the same trick that she used to play on her father whenever she wanted to go out to party with her friends. Juliette heard her mother say those words to her through her tears and she asked her mother if it was really her? Mrs. Harper said, yes it is me my baby girl and both in tears hugged and kissed each other. Juliette said to her before I believe that you are my mother, tell me what happened the last time that we are together.

Mrs. Harper told her everything and including them making their favourite meals together.

Juliette embraced and kissed her mother again and Juliette went to the dinner table where her mother kept all the favourite meals that she made for her and she starts eating them all one by one. Mrs. Harper joined her daughter at the dinner table and they both eat together.

After the meal, Juliette asked her mother to tell her all the details of what happened to her on the mission, and how she managed to convince everyone that she was dead.

Mrs. Harper told Juliette what happened in Ukraine concerning her mission there, what she was doing for the past 10 years, the places that she had travelled to. Mrs Harper told Juliette that her father was the love of her life that she has never dated anyone but if she saw a guy that she liked that she was going to have a one night stand with him. The next day everyone would be going their separate ways Juliette shouts "mama" and she asked her what? And Juliette said, nothing mother.

Juliette was about to tell her mother about her life for the past ten years and her mother said to her that she knows everything that has happened to her in the past ten years. Juliette in shock asked her, how did you know everything that has happened in my life for the past ten years' mother?

She brought out a bag that was full of Juliette's pictures and showed it to her and those pictures displayed Juliette at her father's funeral and as well as Juliette's wedding pictures. Juliette was shocked asked her mother how she got all those pictures. Mrs. Harper said to her that it was part of the deals that she made with her targets. Juliette embrace and kissed her again and said "I love you mother"

Mrs. Harper replied back saying, "I love you my baby girl" and Juliette laughed and said to Mrs. Harper, mother I am no longer a little girl.

Mrs. Harper asked if you are not a little girl anymore, how did you end up with the most wanted man in the United States of America.

Juliette tried to defend Bryan but to her surprise, Mrs. Harper said to her that she knew that Bryan was innocent and that all those accusations against Bryan were false. Ms Harper went on to say that, that is what happens when the CIA has some leverage against someone. The CIA uses the people that they have leverage against as the pets and once they are done with them, they will hand them over to the vultures.

Mrs Harper said to Juliette that she thought that she made her a promise not to go after the CIA no matter what the reason Mrs Harpers question was because she heard from one of her contacts that Juliette and her friend were investigating the CIA. Juliette answered mother and said I could help it and sit down and watch when I knew full well that the CIA had something to do about your death It is the same as you when you couldn't help it when you heard about me getting arrested. I guess now you know who I inherited it from.

They laughed together and she said like mother like daughter. Juliette said to her mother that she needed to help her find her husband because ever since this whole incident occurred she hasn't heard from Bryan. Mrs. Harper said to Juliette let us take tonight and enjoy the mother and daughter moment while it lasts as tomorrow they plan on finding her husband Bryan.

# 6 - THE PRIZES

Mrs. Harper contacted one of her contacts who might know what could have happened to Bryan, who might have him in their possession and the location that they might be keeping him in. Her contact told her that a few weeks ago that some members of the Russian mafia came to him and asked him the same questions. The contact asked the mafia what did Bryan do to them and why are they looking for him so badly? But they gave him no answers and they all drove away immediately.

Whatever Bryan might have done to those Russians the contact doubted that Bryan was still alive.

Mrs. Harper asked her contact to send her, the location of the Russian mafia if he knew.

He told her that she should give him some time so that he can contact one of his associates who might know the Russian's location.

Mrs. Harper said to him that she will wait for him to send her the pin of their locations.

Her contact did not bother to ask her what was going on or why was she looking for Bryan's locations because he knew already. He knew that Bryan was her son-in-law and that he was the one who had been updating her about what was going on in Juliette's life and that he was the one that took all those pictures for her.

Juliette woke up, rose from her bed and came downstairs where her mother was and kissed her and greeted her.

Mrs. Harper greeted her back and they both asked each other whether they had a good night's rest or not.

Juliette said to her that she couldn't sleep. She was turning over and over all around her bed and she was worrying the whole night about what might happen to her husband. The only time that she managed to get some sleep was after she took some sleeping tablets.

Mrs. Harper asked her whether she really loved him.

Juliette replied back to her mother that she really loved him so much.

Mrs. Harper said to her daughter that she knew exactly how she was feeling right now, that she also felt the same way any time she was away from her and her father.

And that's why she had been up all night, talking to all her contacts to see if anyone knew about her husband's location or what might have happened to him.

Juliette asked her if anything had come up yet?

She said, yes and that she was still waiting for them to send her his location pin.

Her contact eventually sent her the pin to the location of the Russians. He sent her a second text apologising to her for not informing her that the Russians were looking for her son-in-law. It was part of a deal they had, that as Bryan was her son-in-law, should anything happen that might endanger Bryan could also endanger her daughter.

Mrs. Harper told Juliette that her contacts have sent her the pin of Bryan's location.

She should take a backseat while she goes and surveys the location. She will find out where it is and how to get in because the people that have him in their possession are extremely dangerous.

Juliette asked her, mother which people was she talking about?

She replied the Russians.

Juliette asked her what business does her husband have with the Russians that will make them have him in their possession because she can't remember Bryan telling her anything about having any business with the Russians.

Mrs. Harper said to her that's why she was asking her to sit back while she goes and surveys the location. Once she comes back, she can plan her next move which will be about breaking Bryan out from the possession of the Russians.

Juliette replied that there is no way that she is going to sit back and wait for her to return and she asked her, ok now what if my husband is in there with the Russians? Who was she going to say to him that she was?

Because as far as Bryan's concerned all he knows is that you are dead and how much time did she think that she was going to have to explain everything to him.

Mrs. Harper said to her that she has a point, but she would still have to take a back seat in the boat and wait for her. Mrs. Harper will go in alone and survey the place because the pin that she has was saying that their location is an island.

The island is fifteen minutes away from the forest that they are in.

They were getting ready to make their way to the Russians location. Juliette was waiting, expecting her mother to bring out some guns and grenades from a storeroom only to see her mother coming out with torches, a rope and the equipment she was going to use to survey the location.

She asked her mother if this was all we are going to need for the mission?

Her mother replied back to her, yes that was all she was going to need to break her husband out from the Russians possession.

Juliette asked her what about guns and grenades?

She asked her back, what about them?

Juliette replied back to her mother saying are we not going to use them for this mission?

Mrs. Harper replied that there was no 'we' in this mission. That you are going to sit in the boat and wait since she didn't want to wait inside the house. And she also laughed at her and said, when we get there and if her husband was there, she thinks that they will start shooting and throwing grenades at the Russians? This was not a movie that she can see that she used to watch a lot of action movies but to remind herself that this is real life, not an action movie.

All she needed to do was to locate Bryan with Russians so can she see what her mother was capable of doing. Mrs. Harper only used a bomb to destroy the federal agent's convoys because she needed to create a diversion for herself because they were on the move. But this time it was different and Juliette was so excited to be part of the mission with her mother.

They piloted the boat to the island, stopping a short swim away from the island. Both Juliette and Mrs. Harper wearing wet suits. Mrs. Harper jumped into the cold water and swam to the island, leaving Juliette alone in the boat.

Meanwhile, Mr. Viktor and some of his men were making their way off the island to go and search for Juliette. They spotted a boat parked right in the middle of the sea and that boat was trespassing because that island was a private island. Mr Viktor steered his boat towards the trespasser.

Juliette had sneaked one gun aboard with her, but the guns that the Russians had far outnumbered hers.

Mr. Viktor shouted over from his boat to ask her what she was doing here at this time all alone?

Juliette explained that because it was in the evening time that she and her mother went to that island.

Mr. Viktor and his men, on the other hand, were leaving at that time because it was much easier for them to travel inside the city during the night hours.

Mr. Viktor did not know that it was Juliette, the very reason they were going to search in the city in the first place. Her face was painted all in green.

Juliette lied to him by saying that she was lost in the middle of the sea. She had sailed all around the sea to find her way out.

He said to her but we saw your boat parked right here from when we left shore.

She replied that she parked here because she was tired from driving the whole evening trying to find her way out.

But Mr. Viktor knew that she was lying and he boarded her boat and took her with him. He ordered some of his men to take Juliette's boat and drive around the island to see whether they will find her mother.

Mrs. Harper climbed onto the island and was trying to jam the security alarms, only for her to see the Russians returning with her daughter.

Mr. Viktor boat was in the last boat accompanied only by two of his men. Mrs. Harper knew immediately that was their boss because her contact also sent her his picture.

Creeping through the bush, she quietly waited for them to drive up by the seashore. She immediately puts his two men to sleep, taking their guns and grenades. Mr. Viktor lunges at her, but she kicks him swiftly, breaking one of his arms, his left arm that he loved so much.

So she takes him with her immediately and she told him to ask his men to open the gates. But he refuses so she twists his broken arm more. The pain was too much so he told his men to open the gates. Mrs. Harper followed him in and demanded that his men gave her daughter back to her or she was going to kill them all.

Mr. Viktor said that they should shoot her because she was bluffing.

She shot three of his men in their legs at the same time, to show them that she was not bluffing.

She said to them that their boss was going to be next. She was going to remove the pin from a grenade and put it inside their boss's mouth if they still refused to give back her daughter to her.

Bryan heard three gunshots and quickly came out to see what was going on outside, only to find his wife outside.

Bryan said that he didn't know what was going on here but everyone has to calm down because they all started off on the wrong feet. He snatched his wife away from the person that was holding her and begged Mr.

Viktor to order his men to drop their weapons. This was his wife, Juliette, that he and his men were going out to search for.

Mr. Viktor ordered his men to drop their weapons and Juliette begged her mother to let go of Mr. Viktor and her mother let him go. So Mr. Viktor, now furious went inside with his men.

Juliette asked Bryan how he recognised that it was her even though she painted her face with some green paint.

Bryan replied back to her that did she remember one day when he was teaching her how soldiers used to invade their targets on the battlefield and Juliette said yes that she remembered how she painted his face and he painted hers in green paint.

Bryan asked her who that lady was standing there and where did she find her?

Juliette said to him, that lady standing there was my mother.

Bryan asked her your stepmother or what? And Juliette replied back to him, my real mother the one that I told you who died ten years ago. Juliette introduced Bryan to her mother and she told Bryan that she was going to tell him everything in the morning that right now all she needed was to get some sleep.

Mrs. Harper was about to leave but Bryan begged her to spend the night with them at the island and that him and her had a lot of catching up to do. Mrs. Harper asked her what about the Russians?

Bryan told her that he was going to talk to them. Bryan took Mrs. Harper with him and went into the place that Mr. Viktor and his men were.

Mr. Viktor asked Bryan if he brought Mrs. Harper here so that she can finish him off?

Bryan said, no. He brought her with him to formally introduce who she was to him, that she is his mother-in-law.

Mr. Viktor told him that he's not going to be part of their little family reunion, that all he needed from him was for Bryan to tell him what is really going on. If this lady standing here, that we thought was responsible for my son's murder was your mother-in-law, then who was responsible for my son's death?

Bryan replies to him that was why he brought in his mother-in-law with him, so they all can figure out who was responsible for his son death.

Mr. Viktor said, never! There was no way he is going to work with this American woman, that he only agreed to work with Bryan because he felt sorry for him and also that he saw what his people were trying to do to him. But for this woman, never. Even though it will take him many years to find his son's killers, he was willing to wait.

Mrs. Harper said the same thing. There is no way that she was going to team up and work with the Russians. She only came here to find him because of her daughter and that now that they have found him, her mission is done.

She was about to leave until Bryan begged her to stay and since he no longer had any team – all his team members were dead and he promised Mr. Viktor that he was going to help him find his son's killers, once he helped him locate his wife. He intended to keep the promise that he made to him.

He continued by saying he needed her to please help him out since he can't go outside because of what happened.

She asked Bryan which of his team members were dead?

Bryan showed her their picture.

She told him that none of them was dead. They were all still alive.

Bryan was shocked told her that he watched on the news and he saw for himself how they buried all of them.

She told him that in the same way, they all thought that she was dead. She said she will call one of her contacts and ask them to send her pictures with the time and date of his friend's capture.

But while they waited for her contact to send his friend's pictures she said Bryan should tell her what happened to Mr. Viktor's son and why did they think that she was the one that murder his son.

Bryan told her everything, and she told him that the only ones who were capable of carrying such an attack out on Mr. Viktor and his son were the CIA agents. Her contact texted her the pictures of Bryan's friends and Bryan saw it and confirmed for himself that his friends were still alive and that Ms. Sophia just played him.

Mrs. Harper told him, looking at what Ms. Sophia did to him and his friends that she must be the one responsible for what happened to Mr. Viktor's son because she was extremely dangerous. One of her contacts told her that some of the CIA agents were planning something extremely dangerous but she paid no attention to it because she wanted nothing to do with the CIA again.

So Bryan went in and told Mr. Viktor that he has found out who was responsible for his son's death.

Mr. Viktor asked who? Did your mother-in-law finally confess that she did it?

Bryan said no, it was his mother-in-law who figured out who did it and that it was the deputy director of the CIA that attacked his place and murder his son.

Mr. Viktor was furious called all his men out for them to go and find Ms. Sophia and kill her. But Mrs. Harper laughed at him and said you Russians! Look at me. I have been off the field for the past ten years and look at what I was able to do to you and your men! Let alone a whole current deputy director of the CIA. Okay, let me ask you this; when you and your men get to the CIA headquarters what are you going to do? Walk in with your men and shoot all the CIA agents. And even if you managed to get to her that she will kill you all, all by herself.

That, that lady is nobody you Russians wants to mess with. And the act of the Russians attacking CIA agents will be an act that will lead to wars between Russia and America. That she expected him to do much better but, well, what can one expect from the Russians other than war.

So Bryan said that that's why both of them need to put their difference aside and work together to find his friends because Ronald has some evidence that they can use to take down Ms. Sophia and her team.

And that now it all makes sense to him why his friends betrayed him and none of them will get what they want. Unless they all work together and help him find his friends before anyone finds them. And to you, Mr. Viktor, even though you won't kill her, with this evidence you can get justice for your son. And to you, Mrs. Harper, by helping find his friends, and using this evidence, she can get revenge for what the CIA did to you by exposing Ms. Sophia and the people that are working with her.

That he needs them to please put their difference aside and work together. Even if she won't do it for him that she does it because of her daughter because he needs to clear his name and his wife name so both of them will be able to build up their own family, which they won't be able to do if they are always watching behind their shoulders.

Both Mrs. Harper and Mr. Viktor agreed to work together for the sake of their children to find Bryan's friends.

Meanwhile, Bryan's friends were in the place that those agents kept them, and were trying all they could to locate Bryan. All they noticed was a parked car with two people inside that had been following them everywhere they went. They said to each other that once they locate Bryan's location, they are going to first kill those two people because they know that it was Ms. Sophia that send them to monitor all their movements.

And once that they finished killing them, they are going to leave everything that Ms. Sophia gave them - including the money - behind.

And Ronald told them that they need to go to the gas stations and make sure that they are caught on cameras so it will be easy for Bryan to locate them. And they all did so and Mrs. Harper and Mr. Viktor with some of his men were able to locate Bryan's friends. And they followed Bryan's friends to their hotel noticing that there was a black van following Bryan's friends.

Mrs. Harper said that those people inside that van were sent by Ms. Sophia so they can monitor Bryan's friends. Once Bryan's friends find him, they are either going to kill them and alert Ms. Sophia to Bryan's location or they will alert her of all their locations.

So she said, here's what's going to happen; you and your men will follow Bryan's friends and blindfold and kidnap them and take them to the island where Bryan is. Make sure that they don't have any devices on them whether it's cell phones or anything while she deals with these people inside the black van to see whether there were any other people that she sent to watch them or whether it was just those.

Mr. Viktor and his men did as they were told and Mrs. Harper created a diversion and shot everyone inside the black van making it look like they were robbed.

Mrs, Harper travelled to the island and she made sure that nobody was following her.

Meanwhile, Bryan's friends were screaming and asking for help only for the blindfolds to be removed from their faces. They found Bryan standing in front of them. At first, they thought Bryan was going to kill them for what they did to him and they started begging him to forgive and spare their lives, it was Ms. Sophia that told them to do so, so she can help them escape the prison sentence by faking their death.

Bryan laughed and embraced and told them that he knew everything that happened, that they were brothers and that he was so excited when he heard that they were still alive, that he was the one that asked for help to find you guys.

They all reconciled with each other and Bryan introduced everyone to them and told them how he came to be working with the Russians. His friends told their own stories. And they all welcomed each other and Bryan called them all to order.

He said that if there was anything like fate, that it was fate that brought each one of them together and starting from today onwards that they are all one family Russians or not, American or not that they are all a family the group rejoiced and partied together.

Mrs. Harper went to Mr. Viktor and apologised to him for breaking one of his arms.

He said to her that it's fine and he would have done the same thing to save Igor his son. They both laughed and said to each other that's what parenting is all about.

Waking up the next morning, Bryan's called everyone all together as one family. He asked Ronald if he still has the evidence he has been keeping so they can use it to expose Ms. Sophia and the people that are helping her out and get justice for the death of Mr. Viktor's son. Ronald said yes.

Meanwhile, Juliette saw an announcement on the news that Ms. Sophia is the new director of the CIA. She turned up the volume of the TV and everyone in the room watched what was going on.

Mrs. Harper said to them that even due that they have the evidence, it will no longer be valid now that Ms. Sophia is the new director of the CIA. She was going to do anything to make sure that the evidence is seen as being fabricated. It will be dismissed because it came from the wrong source, that it will lead back to you Bryan that you fabricated the evidence now that she is the CIA director and used it to clear your name.

Ms. Sophia has outplayed you at every turn, but he should not lose hope yet. Since his friends said that she was hiding them inside a dark site, that means she is planning something extremely dangerous inside that dark site. All they need to do right now is to use all the resources they have to locate that dark site and use it to expose her. To Mr. Viktor, she said that he might locate her there all alone because she doubts that the other CIA agents know about the dark site.

Meanwhile, Ms. Sophia the night before she became the director of the CIA, was invited out by her boss to dinner. Over dinner, her boss told her everything about him and how he found her and also the reasons why she doesn't recognise who he was. Agent Mike who was the CIA director said to her that it is time for him to retire and he's happy that he was the one that found her and he's also happy that he's leaving the CIA agents in good hands. Looking at how she handled Bryan's case and the other cases that she had been handling, he knew that it was time for him to retire and let a new agent with new experience lead the CIA agents. He was not trying to say that he's too old and they both laughed. He asked Ms. Sophia whether she will do him the honour and accept to be the new CIA director?

Ms. Sophia pretends and asked him, whether he was asking her or telling her?

The CIA director said that he was asking her to do him the honour and be the new CIA director.

Ms. Sophia accepted his offer.

The reason she pretended she did not want the position was that she did not want to seem like she was dying to have that his position and be the new CIA director.

They embraced each other and Ms. Sophia called Robert to share the good news with him. But Robert told her that his boss also called him and asked him out for a dinner and told him during their dinner that he wanted him to become the new chief of staff of the DEA.

Ms. Sophia asked him what was his response.

He replied that he pretended to be in shock to hear that news. And Ms. Sophia also said the same to him. Robert invited her out that the same night and she went to meet him. And he asked what was going to happen if their bosses did not retire by themselves? because he hasn't figured out yet how they are going to use Bryan and his friends to get what they want.

She answered him that she was planning to use Bryan's case to force both their bosses into agreeing to early retirements until the Russians move into the States. It changed and made her plans much easier and that's one of the reasons why they are building all that equipment at the dark site. Once it's ready to be used she was going to use it to eliminate both of them. She also told him that they need to go home and get some sleep and prepare for what is ahead of them tomorrow. Once both are sworn in as the heads of their offices they are going to invite the others, so they can all celebrate together. After their celebration, in the morning that they are going to plan how they are going to help Richard get what he wanted and help Charles to run for the DA's office.

And he asked her, what of Mr. William?

She replied that once Richard becomes the commissioner of IRS then everything is settled. After both were sworn in and after their celebration party, Ms. Sophia, without wasting any time, called everyone together.

She said to them, that here is what is going to happen because she needs to go to work early to make a good first impression as the newly appointed director of the CIA and that Robert should also do the same because it was his first day. A good impression as a boss will send some messages to the other agents where you are planning to lead them to.

That they are going to set the current IRS commissioner up and send him to early retirement because he will have only two choices they are going to give him. Either he retires or he's going to serve a long time inside a federal prison. And whichever one he chooses to take, with the evidence she had against him he will be coming out of the IRS office. The polls were looking so good for Charles after he won that case at the federal high court, that his opponents stood no chance against him.

Once Richard becomes the IRS commissioner he is going to set up an offshore account for Mr. William and make all his assets tax-free. And she told them the plans of how to set the current commissioner of the IRS up and she also told them that everyone needs to play their parts very well for this plan to work. And they succeeded in setting the current commissioner up when she finds lots of assets and money linked up to him.

So then Ms. Sophia arrested him without wasting much time before other federal agents had the chance to start snooping around. She arrested the current commissioner of the IRS and said to him with the evidence she has against him, no lawyers can save him from her but looking at all the good work he has done for America, a man like him needs to go down with honour, he needs to be offered a deal. If she didn't offer him a deal, what did he think would happen to him when he's inside prison with all the people that he has been sending to prison. How long did he think that he's going to last inside prison before someone killed him?

But before she presents any deals to him, she needs one of his lawyers to be present.

He requested for one of his lawyers and she presented the deals to him and his lawyer was to choose whichever one would be best for him. She continued by saying to his lawyer that he should advise his client that she is giving them only thirty minutes to decide which one will be good for him.

And the reason why she made sure that his lawyer was present and partaking in the deals was that she does not want to make it seems like he accepted the deals without the consent of his legal advisor.

She came back after thirty minutes and brought out her handcuffs, but they told her to wait and his lawyer said to her that his client chooses the option of retiring as the commissioner of the IRS. She told them to put it in writing and he should make a public statement about his retirement which they agreed and to do as they were told. Richard became the new commissioner of the IRS because he was next in line to take up that position.

Charles won his election and becomes the newly elected DA, while Richard set up offshore accounts and made all Mr. William's assets tax-free and they all got what they wanted. After their celebration party, Ms. Sophia went back to her place with Robert.

# 7 - IT IS OUR WORLD NOW

Ms. Sophia woke Robert up from her bed and said to him, it is time that he gets dressed and come downstairs so they can discuss their next plan, now that everything inside the new site is ready for launching, they need to get on with their next plans.

Robert said to her, must everything about her have to do with work? Why can they not be just for a moment, who they really are and have some fun together?

Ms. Sophia said to him, that she doesn't want him to get any wrong ideas into his head about what just happened between them last night, that it was never a thing and that it will never become a thing.

So Robert said to her, okay that he also wants to verify what happened between them last night but it seems like it was just his imagination that was disturbing him. Now that she has cleared the air about how things stand between them, he has to get rid of it and get on with it.

She said to him, you better do and get rid of all those ideas from his imagination.

So Robert freshened up and came downstairs and he asked her, so what's our next plan going look like or going to be?

So she said to him that their next plan was going to be so diplomatic that they cannot afford to make any mistakes.

Robert said to her, must I be worried because it sounds like it was going to be extremely dangerous.

She replied, yes it was going to be more tactical and also extremely dangerous that's why they can't afford to make any mistakes, that why the two of them only will carry out the plan and give the others updates only.

So Robert said to her, okay whatever she was planning he is in, no matter how tactical and extremely dangerous that it will be. He asked her about her plan.

She said to him that now everything inside the new site is ready for launching after five years of failing and trying again that their teams have finally created the software that they needed and now it time to get all of them tested. That they are going to step up a meeting and invite five of the eight military generals whose nations have the missile defence system. They will get them to hand over the codes of their missile defence system.

She was going to represent America as their military general.

Robert asked her, what about the American military generals? How was she going to replace her?

She asked him what about her? Did she need to remind him that she was their director again?

And she said to him since it seems like you have forgotten so soon after what just happened between us last night. She is the CIA director, which means she is in charge of the nation's security both at home and overseas. And in that meeting, the reason why she won't invite Russia and United Kingdom's military generals was that she has other plans for them.

But as for the other five military generals they invited, if any one of them agrees to sign off their missile defence systems to her, their nations will be saved from what was going to happen. But their military generals will die for their nations after the meeting. While the nations will be saved, the ones that refused to sign over their missile defence systems to her that they are going to die and their nations will have been ruined.

And as for Russia and the United Kingdom here was the plans she had in mind for them. At exactly 2:15 AM in Russia while it's exactly 12:15 AM in the United Kingdom she was going to send a virus into the British missile defence systems and cause it to have systems malfunctions that will weaken their missile defence system, so they can send in a Russian missile after they have caused the Russia missile to malfunction and send it to destroy the London bridges and some building close to the London bridges. People are going to die but they're part of collateral damage. At exactly 10:15 AM in Russia and exactly 8:15 AM in Britain they are going to call and explode five Russian top government officials including their military general, their president chief of staff and the three others but all this will happen once the London bridges collapse so that it will seem like the Russians attacked the United Kingdom and the United Kingdom retaliated by killing their government officials after they found out that the missile that bombed the London bridge came from Russia. But all things will have happened once and there will be chaos all over Asia, Europe and the Middle East when the British agents call her to find out what's going on and who did she thinks is responsible for these attacks.

But firstly, they needed to set up a meeting with the military generals to see which one nation to spare and which nations to ruin. Secondly, they were going to set up another meeting with the others at the dark site and update them about their next plan before they carry on with the attacks. Once the attacks between Russia and the United Kingdom have been done, then Madam President will try to restore some peace between the two nations by calling both the Russian president and the British prime minister on a conference call informing them about how she was going to help them find who was responsible for the attacks. Since neither country would admit responsibility for the attacks.

Because those two nation's leaders will be threatening to go to war against each other and Madam President will try anything in her power to make sure that war is avoided, but she was going to ask them to give her more time to find out who is responsible for those attacks. And Madam President will have called and set up a meeting inside the Situations Room to help Russia and Britain to find out who was responsible for those attacks.

But she will tell her that her main concern, for now, should not be about those two nations but instead, should be about America's missile defence systems. She knows what will happen if America's missile defence systems were weaker or if any of America's missiles have been hacked through a systems malfunction virus that has been going through other nations in the world. Any nation that the American missiles will attack will have half their cities wiped away.

If by any means the American defence system was weaker than their enemies won't waste any time sending in their missiles.

Her main concern should be America and her citizen's safety first and then they can help the other nations out. Once that is done that she will suggest to Madam President that some of the CIA agents will be working together with the defence force to upgrade their nations missile defence systems, while other agents will be working on how to find out who is responsible for those attacks. Once Madam President agrees, they will take Igor and some Russians into the dark site and get some evidence that can be used against them to frame the Russians as a consequence, both America and Britain will go to war against Russia.

Robert asked her with all these attacks she is planning to do, what was in for them? Because he knew what was in it for them for their first plan.

So she said to him that these attacks will help boost their nation's economy and since these nations have missiles defence systems and have been planning for World War III that it's time. She will send them into World War III since none of them were ready for it.

While Europe is in chaos the Euro will fall and in Britain, the Pounds will also fall and he should guess which nation's currencies that will rise high in the market.

And he replied theirs, which is the Dollar.

She said to him, that he sees that he's not that dumb after all. And what was in for them, was that they would not need to send any of their agents into battle anymore. Any of the targets they have are going to sit back in their offices while their targets explode thanks to the bombing phone calls.

And was he not tired of losing some of his good agents during the drugs raids?

And he said that he was and she asked him why then was he asking her what was in for them?

He replied that he just wanted to know and he asked her where the venue was they were going to set up for the meeting with the military generals.

She replied back to him the only location that she knew that was going to be suitable for the meeting was not anywhere near the dark site.

They succeeded in setting up a meeting with the five military generals. Ms. Sophia told the generals what the meeting was all about. Two out of those five generals agreed and assigned their nations missile defence systems over. One of the three who refused to sign said to her that, there is no way that he's going to sign his nation missile defence systems to the Americans.

She replied that this meeting was a peaceful meeting, that everyone was allowed to make their own decision as they thought would be best for their nations. She respects each of them and every one of their decisions when it comes down to their nation's safety. She said to the two other military generals that assigned their nation's missile defence systems to her, good decision to both you generals and that they won't regret it.

Those five military generals left and she said to Robert that now they have what they wanted. They are going to set up a meeting with the others tomorrow at the dark site and inform them about their next plan.

They set up the meeting with the other three at the dark site which they all came and she told them about her next plan. Meanwhile, after the meeting with the military generals, one of Mrs. Harper's contacts texted her. He said that one of his contacts told him that Ms. Sophia, with the DEA chief of staff standing right behind, invited five out of the eight nations that have missile defence systems.

She asked the military generals to sign their missile defence systems over to her. Two agreed and assigned theirs to her, while three refused.

The reason he texted her was that he needs her help because whatever Ms. Sophia was planning to do would shake the whole world and he was worried about his own nation because his nation did not have missiles defence systems. Whatever she finds out she should let him know and he will assist her in whatever ways that he can.

Immediately, Mrs. Harper called everyone to gather together because she has some important information sent to her by one of her contacts.

Whatever Ms. Sophia was planning might lead to World War III and she showed all of them what her contact sent to her.

She asked Bryan if he knew anyone that Ms. Sophia might be working with during the time she was sending him on all those missions. Her intel also told her that she was with the DEA chief of staff in the meeting with the five military generals.

Bryan answered that he did not know anyone besides Ms. Sophia.

So, she told Ronald to see if he was able to hack into Ms. Sophia's phone to see who she has been in contact with during the past 24 hours without her noticing. If she were to find out that she was hacked, she would trace the IP server and it will be over for them once she has their location.

So Ronald told her that he can try but it was going to be 50\50 chance.

Mrs. Harper told him to try and she told everyone to get ready for them to move to another location if Ronald failed in his mission. She also told Ronald to cover the webcam camera so she won't be able to capture his face. He should change his system's real location so it will buy them some time to move to another location.

Ronald managed to hack into Ms. Sophia's phone and he got all the information he needed. The reason why he succeeded was that she was taking a nap at that time and Ms. Sophia didn't like to be disturbed anytime she was taking a nap.

They got the names of Mr. William, Richard and Charles and Bryan's friends recognised Charles's face as he was the attorney that handled their case.

They all found out about the connection they had with Ms. Sophia. Mrs. Harper said for them to take down these four men and Ms. Sophia with them. It was going to be hard because they all were protected by the US government and no one was going to believe their stories because some of them in here are dead to the public, while some are fugitives. The only man who can help them is a Russian and who in their right mind is going to believe a Russian man? Whatever that they need to do to take these people down they are going to do it all by themselves.

They must first find out which of these four men will lead them to their secure site. She asked Ronald to put those men's faces back on the system and their positions. Ronald did as he was told.

Mrs. Harper said looking at all these men that the one who might lead them to the site is Mr. William.

So she asked Ronald to log in and find all the information about Mr. William for her.

The reason she chose Mr. William was that he was a politician and a businessman and won't have time to check his phone or who's watching him because he puts all his trust in the hands of his security and bodyguards to protect him all the time. So Ronald got all the information about Mr. William for her.

She asked him, what is Mr. William's location now?

He told her and she replied that she was going to handle this mission on her own and whatever she finds out she was going to inform them.

And she was going to watch Mr. William until he led her to that secret site of theirs. So, on that day that Mr. William was going to meet up with his other team members at the dark site, Mrs. Harper followed him. But after an hour of driving Mr. William parked at the train station.

Mrs. Harper followed Mr. William from a safe distance so that Mr. William's security guards won't notice that her car has been following them since they started their journey. Mrs. Harper waited at the train station the whole day, but Mr. William did not come back to his convoy. She only saw him walking inside the train station but he never came out again. Eventually, Mrs. Harper saw his convoy leaving without Mr. William inside it, so she decided to drive back to the island.

# 8 - THE LAST MISSION

When Mrs. Harper got to the island she told everyone about what just happened on her mission, so she asked Ronald to find out about any islands or deserts that were close to the train station. She also said that Ms. Sophia was so smart that she covered all her tracks and she said that the only two places that she could hide such a secret site were either under the sea or underground in the desert. Whichever one it was that they needed to find it and use anything inside that secret site to expose her. Ronald hacked the system to see which of the two places were closer to the train station. He found out that the only place that was close to the train station was the desert and there were three deserts nearby.

Mrs. Harper told them that they are going to go to all three of those deserts that were around the train station location to see which one was used to build her secret site and that whichever one it was they were going to make sure that she was inside it. That way, they could tip off the other force units about that location that she was inside it that way the CIA agents could come and arrest all of them.

Meanwhile, after the meeting that Ms. Sophia had with her team was over, she went straight to the new site with Robert. Getting inside the new site with Robert, so she asked the agents that were working on the software to get all the software ready for the launch. When the software was ready for launching, Ms Sophia asked them to bring out all five of the military general's cell phone numbers and they did as they were told. She dialled all of their cellphone numbers at once and the five military general's phones exploded immediately after the call. It was all over the news about how five military generals died in the explosion and the cause of their death was still unknown.

After the phone call bomb explosion, Ms. Sophia told them that should prepare the virus and get them all ready and that they should inform her when it is ready for launching as she is going to use them to cause her targets missile defence systems to malfunction. She said to Robert since the two generals had sacrificed their lives for the nation, therefore their nation will be safe and that their main focus now should be on the ones that refused to assign their missile defence systems to her. While the nations were still trying to find out what was the cause was of their military general's deaths. She stated that she was going to send the virus to their missile defence system so that it will cause it to malfunction. Once that is done, she explained what she was going to cause their neighbouring countries that way some parts of Asia, Europe and the Middle East would be in chaos.

All the attacks should be carried in the afternoon because of the time zone differences. A clear instruction was that it should be carried out at exactly 2:00 PM, Washington DC time, that way it would hit them while some people were still asleep. They informed her that the virus was ready to be launched

She went with Robert and at exactly 2:00 PM Washington DC time she sent out the virus to the nations whose military generals refused to assign their nations missile defence systems to her. The virus could cause those nations missile defence systems to malfunction and they could not control their missiles. Their missile defence systems were alerting them that there was a virus and that they have also lost control over their missiles and their missile defence systems and there was nothing that they can do about it because they could not turn them off.

Immediately some of their missiles went off, while they were still trying to track the location that their missiles were going to. They got alerts on their systems about some incoming missiles from their neighbouring countries and that it was coming towards their country. Their missiles bombed their neighbouring countries cities while their neighbouring countries missiles also bombed and destroyed their own cities.

That was a night that both Asia, Europe and the Middle East would never forget because both their cities and the citizens that were living there were attacked and their countries were ruined. There were mass slaughters and both innocent children and their parent's lost their loved ones. Some children that survived the attack were crying and looking for their parents while some parents were crying and looking for their children.

The attack shocked the whole of Asia, Europe and the Middle East and every nation began preparing for World War III, - that way they wouldn't be the next nation to be attacked. They closed all their borders, both land and sea. None of the nations that were part of the attack seemed to understand what the cause of those attacks was and how some of their missiles went off without anyone controlling them

After Mrs. Harper saw what had happened, she realized why Ms. Sophia needed all those military generals to assign their nation's missiles defence systems to her. The generals who had agreed to assigned their nations missiles defence systems to her, found their nations were safe but as for those military generals who did not agree, disaster had struck.

Mrs. Harper texted all her contacts that she needed them to come and assist her to locate the secret site before Ms. Sophia caused all nations into World War III. She told everyone on the island that they are not going to tip anybody off about that secret site when they find it because there is a change of plan which was once they located the secret site. Ms Harpers plan was that once they located the secret site that they would destroy everything inside of it. Meanwhile, Ms. Sophia received a phone call from the head of MI6 in Britain asking about the attacks that had just happened and who she thought was responsible for them. She told the MI6 agent that she doesn't have anyone in mind yet that might be responsible for all the attacks but she was going to look into it and if she found any leads that she would contact her. Ms Sophia called Robert and said to him that it was time for their next attack which was to cause conflict between the United Kingdom and Russia

At exactly 12:15 AM in the United Kingdom, 2:15 AM Russian time, she sent out the same virus into the British missile defence system which caused their system to malfunction and the British army lost control of their missile defence systems. The Russian army also lost control of their missiles and some of their missiles went off headed straight for London. The British, lost access over their missile defence system, immediately got an alert of incoming missiles heading towards London. They did everything in their power to stop or divert the missiles to the closest desert but they couldn't because the virus had already damaged their missiles control systems What a morning it was for the Londoners and for all the British citizen's. There were tears in the eyes and hearts of the British citizens, there was some togetherness among the British citizens for the very first time for them, they left their political and racial differences aside. They realized that if World War III was about to begin they needed unity.

There was no more sleep both in the eyes of the Londoners and the British citizens as both civilians, police and military help out and save some of the survivors of the missile attack. The main concern at the time was to save the lives of their surviving citizen's. In the morning the British agents would have found out where the missiles had come from and update their prime minister. Both their prime minister and agents will update Buckingham Palace before their prime minister updates the citizens as to who was responsible for the attack on London.

At exactly 8:15 AM United Kingdom time 10:15 AM Russian time, the Russian president lost five of his top cabinet officials in phone call explosions. The British agents found out in the morning that those missiles belonged to Russia. Both the British prime minister and Buckingham Palace wants answers as to why the Russian missiles attacked their nation. The Russian president told the British that his military general reported that they lost control of their missiles through the ongoing virus. Whilst the Russian president was still on the call with the British they informed him about the death of his military generals that just informed him about their missiles early in the morning as well as the death of his chief of staff and three others of his cabinet members

The Russian president was furious and asked the British Prime Minister, who he was still on the phone with was it because of the missile attack that the British wanted revenge for what happened?

The Russian president ended the call and went live on the news immediately to inform all his citizens about what just happened to his cabinets and the missile attack that happened very early in the morning in London, the British prime minister did the same thing. Madam President after hearing the news about what happened in London and in Russia she asked her chief of staff to set up conference calls between the British prime minister and the Russian president because she had to speak with them and try to find a common ground to resolve the issues before both nations go to war with each other. During her conference call with the British prime minister and the Russian president, both nations leaders agreed that they are going to give her 72 hours to find out who was responsible for all the attacks but if any missiles attacked any of their nations before the 72 hours that they gave her that they are going to strike back to any nations that, the missiles were coming from.

Madam President asked her chief of staff to set up another meeting in the Situations Room with all the heads of the military and secret services in the United States of America. Her chief of staff set up the meeting and Madam President told everyone what that meeting was about. Ms. Sophia – being the director of the CIA – stood up and told Madam President about what her main concern should be and what was going to happen if they did not focus on the nation's missile defence systems.

The other heads of force units in America said that they hate to say this but they agree with the CIA director and what she said was the truth.

Madam President asked them what was their advice on what she should do now because she promised the other two nation's leaders that she was going to give them some answers in the next seventy-two hours.

Ms. Sophia stood up again and told Madam President what she thought might be the solution to save both their nations and find some answers of who's responsible for all those attacks so she can inform the two nation's leaders.

So Madam President and some other heads of units agreed with Ms. Sophia's plan being the solution.

At the end of their meeting, Madam President assigned the mission to Ms. Sophia and told her to use all resources available to find out the people who are behind all those attacks and she shouldn't hesitate to call the White House for help, if she ever needs it and that America is counting on her.

After the meeting in the Situations Room, Ms. Sophia went back to the new site where Robert was. Robert asked her if Madam President agreed with her plans?

Ms. Sophia told him he should learn how to have some patience sometimes and she told him about how her meeting at the White House went. Finally, she told him what to do.

He should find some Russian professional software developing engineers together with Igor and blindfold them and plant evidence that they are the ones behind all those missiles and phone bombing attacks. He should then take them to the dark site and once that is complete he should inform her so she can send some of her CIA agents and some other force units into that dark site. Once he has done that, he should go back to the DEA department and carry on with his work so it won't raise any suspicion about his whereabouts. Even though he is now the boss. he needs to show up at work sometimes. She was going to text him if she ever needed him. So they can move on to their next plan, she is going upstairs now to brief her agents on her meeting at the White House and to assign her agents their tasks to perform.

She left and Robert managed to succeed in his mission to scout out some Russian professional software developing engineers. He kidnaps them together with Igor and arranges some evidence to show that they are the ones who have been carrying out the attacks that happened and took them to the dark site.

Meanwhile, on the same day, he took those Russians to the dark site, Bryan discovered that site because he, Mrs. Harper and Mr. Viktor divided themselves into three groups. Using Mrs. Harper's contacts and Mr. Viktor's men shared amongst them so it will be much easier for them to locate the secret site.

Mrs. Harper said to them that whichever group that locates that secret site first should wait and inform the others so that all of them can move in at the same time. The reason why Bryan was able to join them on that mission was that he was wearing a plastic face, disguising his real face.

After Bryan discovered that secret site he informed the others to make their way to him. While he was still in hiding and waiting for the others to arrive, he saw Robert with some other agents driving out from the dark site. Bryan saw the entrance and how to get inside the dark site. When the others came he told them what he saw.

Mrs. Harper said there is no time to wait for them to come back so they can finish them off. Instead, they are going to make their way inside the dark site and destroy all the equipment that Ms. Sophia used to carry out all her attacks and put an end to all of it.

They entered the dark site to see what was inside. The next thing they heard was voices and screaming for help. Robert took them in there. He untied and removed their blindfolds so it seemed like they were working there when the US agents come in. Mrs. Harper and her team were getting to the place where all the Russians were. Mr. Viktor saw his dead son, Igor, alive and Igor saw his dead father alive and they both embraced.

Mrs. Harper asked Mr. Viktor if he knew all these people.

He answered, no, he only knew his son. That this is his dead son Igor that he had been talking about.

Mrs. Harper told them that they need to leave the dark site now because something seems off about all this.

Five minutes after they left the dark site, the US agents came in but they only discovered evidence left there with no one inside that dark site. The reason why Mrs. Harper did discover that evidence first was because the evidence was kept in the other room and there was no time for them to search all the rooms inside that dark site.

The CIA agents told Ms. Sophia about the mission and what they saw inside the dark site.

Ms. Sophia was furious and immediately texted Robert to meet her at the new site. They both met up at the new site and Ms. Sophia was furious and told Robert that he shouldn't waste his time and energy and do as he's told,

It was just a simple task she gave him to do and just because she was not there to tell him what to do, he failed. Instead of thinking about how they are going to move into their next mission, she now has to think about how she was going to clean up all his mess.

Robert told her that he did as she instructed him to do.

She replied that if he did as he was instructed to do, why did those agents not find anyone there?

He answered that it was shocking to him that those agents only found that dark site with the evidence inside but they found no one inside it. He was sure that he left them inside that dark site before he left. Maybe, just maybe, someone discovered the dark site and helped them to escape before those agents got there.

Ms. Sophia said, maybe, just maybe, what he said was the truth then who might be the ones behind it. The only one she could think of now is Bryan and his team. There is going to be a bigger problem for them if Bryan and his team were the ones that found Igor and if Igor was going to tell them everything about how he made all those cell phone nuclear bombings.

Since Bryan and his team want to be the heroes, she was going to make him the number one world enemy and since his team's members were dead to the public, then he will be the one to take the fall all by himself this time. Madam President told her that she shouldn't hesitate to call the White House anytime she needs helps and that now was the right time to call for that help.

She said to Robert that he should hope that her plans work this time because if it doesn't they are going to pause their next plan for now and wait for everything to settle down before carrying on.

She called and set up a meeting with Madam President to brief her on what she had found out so far. She went in and briefed Madam President about the dark site and what the US agents discovered inside it.

Madam President asked her who did she think was behind it?

She answered by asking her if she remembered the fugitive that she declared as America's most wanted.

Madam President said yes, and how could she forget about him.

Ms. Sophia said, very well then. She thought that he was the one behind all these attacks that have been happening and she should think why no one has been able to find him yet.

The reason why they haven't found him was that he had been hiding inside the dark site and she also suspected that some people have been helping him, which was the reason why they couldn't find him.

Madam president said to her that there might be some truth to what she was saying, but they are all based on theories. If she was going to make one of her citizens to be the world number one enemy she needed facts, not theories. When she has some evidence to back up what she was saying then she can look into it but for now, she should make sure that news did not get out of the US and make sure that none of those agents who discovered the dark site says anything about their mission until they are sure who was responsible.

If both the British and the Russian leaders find out that the attack that happened in their nations was carried out from US soil, it might result in another issue. It might seem as though the US was planning on sending both nations into a war with each other.

Madam President asked her if she understood what she meant?

Ms. Sophia answered that she did understand.

Ms. Sophia left and went back to the new site and told Robert that her plan did not work this time and they needed to pause everything for now. They must only go to the new site and monitor how everything was going for now until everything settles down. After Ms. Sophia finished telling Robert about what they were going to do, the next thing they heard were gunshots blazing outside their new site.

Meanwhile, before that gunshot incident started, Bryan, together with his team, Mrs. Harper, Mr. Viktor, Igor and the Russian's they save at the dark site along with Mr. Viktor's men returned to the island.

The reason why Mrs. Harper's contacts did not return with them to the island was because something important came up requiring their attention. They told Mrs. Harper about it and told her to update them if anything happens.

Mr. Viktor and Igor embraced each other and Igor said to his father that he saw him die right in front of his two eyes.

Mr. Viktor said the same thing to him.

Mrs. Harper told them that, that's one of the tactics the CIA uses to capture some of their targets. And she said to Mr. Viktor that the time will come for him and his son to catch up and talk about what happened but right now she needs his son to help them to locate the site that Ms. Sophia used to carry out all her plans.

Mr. Viktor said to his son that he can trust Mrs. Harper. He should not leave any details out concerning what he knows about Ms. Sophia.

So Igor told Mrs. Harper that he was sorry. If he had known that his father was still alive, he wouldn't have agreed to develop that cell phone call bomb for Ms. Sophia. The reason he agreed to work with her was that she promised him that once the cell phone call bomb was ready she was going to help him by using it to destroy all the people that were behind his father's death. But he only found out now that Ms. Sophia used him.

Mrs. Harper answered him by saying that's the CIA for you but now was not the time for self-pity and blames.

Mrs. Harper asked him, what else were the men he was working with developing with? And what else was inside that site?

Igor answered by saying that today was the first day that he had ever met these men and that he doesn't know what else MS. Sophia was developing or what was inside that site. He was only allowed to go to his developing rooms where he was creating the cell phone call bomb.

Mrs. Harper called one of the men and asked him what his profession was.

He answered that he's a software developing engineer.

She said to him that he can go and turned to Mr. Viktor and told him that it all makes sense to her now. The reason why Ms. Sophia left these men together with his son at the dark site, as if those American agents found them inside that dark site and they are all Russians, that it was going to seem like the Russians were the ones behind all those attacks that have been happening and they are using America soil to carry out their attacks.

It would then lead to Madam President giving an order that will start a war between Russia on one side and Britain and America on the other. So she asked Igor again, how did the site and the people inside it look?

Igor answered her by saying that there were lots of software engineers and hacks and supervised by many fighting agents inside that site, who never let them leaves that site. The only places they were allowed to use were their rooms, kitchens and the developing rooms. The place looked like it was in turmoil. It seems like it was underground even though it was inside a building. They were never allowed to talk to each other, he only saw them. The reason why he told her earlier that he didn't know if Ms. Sophia was developing anything else inside that site was that he only focussed on how to finish developing the cell phone call bomb so he can use it to avenge his father's death. He was sorry that he was only telling her now. Both their security CCTV cameras and their agents were uptight.

Mrs. Harper said to him that she understood his reason for only telling her now and if what she was thinking was true, then the only place that she can think of right now was the CIA headquarters but it was just a theory. After World War II, the CIA built an underground bunker inside their headquarters that could be used for torture and to eliminate their targets. It was also a hiding place built for their agents if there might be another war.

She was investigating it at the time she was still working as one of the CIA agents and that's why the CIA want her dead so badly. It will be a good hideout site for Ms. Sophia because nobody will suspect her or the CIA headquarters to be used whilst carrying out such a mission.

She asked Ronald to try to search the CIA headquarters archives to find out what it looks like between the nineteen-fifties and the nineteen-seventies and what was there before the city development began.

Ronald did as he was told but only could only find pictures of the CIA headquarters that were uploaded in the nineteen-eighties so she made some drawings on her own based on what she discovered through her investigation before she went into hiding to see if anything might stand out from the pictures Ronald got.

She discovered that something stood out from the ones on the computers; there was another entrance away from the CIA headquarters building, that there was another secret entrance outside the city that might lead right inside the CIA headquarters. Ronald brought up the map of the CIA headquarters on his computer.

Mrs. Harper studied it and used it to point out how they are going to get inside the CIA headquarters without anyone noticing them.

Mrs. Harper said to Mr. Viktor now that he found out that his son was still alive, what was he going to do now? Was he still going to help them or what?

Mr. Viktor answered her by saying even though he has found out that his son was still alive, it won't stop him from helping them out because they are all now a family and that a family sticks together for better or for worse. He and his men are going to represent their motherland and fight for Russia since Ms. Sophia's plan all along was to use his own son to cause a war between Russia and America. He was going to show her that nobody, I said nobody will mess with me or my family and get away scot-free. He is fighting for both his family and his mother nation – Russia. All his men shout "yes we are ready to fight or die for our motherland Russia."

So Mrs. Harper said to them, very well then let's do this and she drew out their plans as to how they were going to attack. She said to them, if anyone of them wants to walk away from this mission then now is the right time to do so. She wouldn't blame anyone for walking away because this mission is going to be a suicide mission and she is not sure if any of them will make it out alive.

Because she doesn't know what kind of things were inside that site, the numbers of the agents or the number of weapons that were inside. They all should know that Ms. Sophia is extremely dangerous and they should approach her with caution.

She said to George and Kenneth that she is going to need them to go and find some pigs and wait for her at the location that she was going to send to them and she was going to tell them what to do with those pigs.

She told Igor that she was going to need him to come with a bazooka and missiles. Once they are by the CIA building's east corner, shots a missile towards one of the US navy's warship, but miss. Once the US navy detects the incoming missile, then he should leave it for the navy to control so that they can send it to a harmless location. Once the US navy detects the missile they will trace the exact location that the missile was coming from and they will alert the other American force units to that exact location. Then he should shoot that bazooka at the entrance and then leave immediately because if any American force units find him there that they will kill him and he will die for real this time.

She said to Ronald that he has a bigger role to play than anyone in this mission. He should make sure that he controls that missile to pass by the US navy's warship and to make sure that they detect it and once they do that he should alert Igor immediately so he can shoot the bazooka and leave immediately.

She also said to Ronald that he should remember that he is also going to be their eyes to tell them what lies ahead of them and which way to take. The CCTV cameras that the CIA agents used to secure their premises were different from any other CCTV cameras in that they turn every two seconds and can also detect any incoming contact to its locations. They are going to use those pigs to create a diversion for themselves so that those CCTV cameras inside the building will detect them and alert those agents inside will be focussed on the chaos, Ronald will have just one minute to hack into their security cameras systems and make it blackout so they can make their way outside the east corner door.

Once Igor shoots that bazooka at the door to the entrance, it will trigger the whole alarm system inside the site and while those agents are trying to find out what was going on that they are going to throw as much tear gas as they could carry. Then they must put their masks on and wait by the next corridor and see what happens next.

They all should pray and hope that the US navy detects the missile and alerts the other US force units and for the US force units to arrive at the site on time because if they don't none of them were going to make it out alive.

She said to Bryan that once they make it to the corridor then he and George with some of Viktor's men will follow her while Viktor with some more of his men will move on to the next corridor since none of her contacts was available now and the only hope they had now was for the US force units to come to the rescue.

Juliette called her mother aside and asked her to promise that she was going to do everything in her power to make sure that Bryan makes it out of the mission alive.

Mrs. Harper told her that she can't make such a promise to her because she didn't know what lies ahead of them and that she won't lie to her.

So Mrs. Harper asked Juliette why was she so anxious for her to make her promise for her husband to make it out alive. What was going on?

Juliette said to her, mother I think that we might be expecting a baby but she's still not sure yet. If she told her husband about it, he might not agree to go with you guys again.

Mrs. Harper said to her daughter that now she understands her reason. She is going to try and make sure her husband makes it out alive.

They all left the island leaving Juliette and Jason behind. When they got to the east corner entrance of the CIA headquarters everyone waited. Mrs. Harper told George and Kenneth to send in the pigs and Kenneth should wait behind so he can drive out with Igor and go somewhere safe and wait for her call.

Ms. Sophia, after hearing that shooting outside the new site, went downstairs immediately with Robert and she asked him to show her all their security cameras and what her agents were shooting at. She called in some of her agents to go outside and check what was going on. She saw on the CCTV cameras that some of her agents were shooting at pigs because those CCTV cameras inside the site detected the pigs.

Ms. Sophia said that something seems to be off here. How can some pigs appear from the middle of nowhere and get to this site because there was no farm around the premises? And she orders all her agents in charge of the CCTV cameras to show her every angle of each of their CCTV cameras They did and they found out that some of their CCTV cameras were blacked out.

She said that someone used those pigs to create a diversion to get inside the site. She alerted all of the agents to be on high alert. And the next thing they heard was the sound of a bazooka that destroyed the east corner door.

After hearing the sounds of the bazooka attack, they saw smoke everywhere, Tear gas canisters were thrown in and the next thing that they saw was people throwing in grenades and bullets raining down on them. There was chaos everywhere.

Ms. Sophia ran to another room with Robert The attacks had caught her off guard., She asked Robert what was going on and told him they should wait inside this room to see what happens next. They didn't have a mask with them and didn't want to go out in case the tear gas hampered their sight and they were shot.

George saw Ms. Sophia and Robert while they were running to that room. He pointed this out to Bryan and Mrs. Harper.

George, without hesitation, ran off leaving Bryan and Mrs. Harper behind and broke down the door to the room and went in immediately, while Bryan and Mrs. Harper were still trying to catch up. George, in a rage, flew at Ms Sophia and attacked her. Ms. Sophia killed him immediately on the spot.

When Bryan and Mrs. Harper finally got inside the room, they both saw George lying dead on the floor while Ms. Sophia was seated on a chair with both her legs on top of George's dead body.

Bryan immediately wants to attack Ms. Sophia but Mrs. Harper held him back.

Ms. Sophia laughed and said to them that now all her theories were true. She turned to Robert and said that this was agent Knox that she told him about, the one that was responsible for those attacks that happened on that day they moved Juliette's location.

So Robert said to her oh! This was the CIA agent that you told me about. So, she is back from the land of the dead to the land of the living.

Ms. Sophia laughed and said to him we are about to find out. She asked Bryan what was he going to do if agent Knox did not hold him back? His dead body would be lying next to his friend's dead body. And she turned to Mrs.

Harper, formerly agent Knox, and said to her that she once admired all the good work she did when she was still working as a CIA agent but this fight had nothing to do with her. This is not the right time for her and her son-in-law trying to be an American hero because she didn't see anything wrong in what she was doing, since some world leaders were busy developing and buying nuclear bombs, missiles, weapons etc using a lot of their nation's annual budgets. They are storing them in case of World War III. Since they didn't know when it's going to happen that it is time she started it for them.

She asked agent Knox what did she think?

But agent Knox never said a word to her.

She told agent Knox that she doesn't have to say anything because she knew already what she was doing was for a good cause. Ms Sophia was going to respect and honour her by calling her agents to stand down. Agent Knox should then ask her men to stand down so they all can leave unharmed.

Mrs. Harper said to her that it has been a while since anyone called her by the name 'Agent Knox' and since she said that she once admired her that means she knows what she is capable of.

Ms. Sophia answered that she knew what she was capable but that wasn't the reason why she was offering a deal to walk free but because she had read all her files and that she saw the same people that she is about to die for, did to her.

Agent Knox said to her, enough of your pep talk that they should get on with it and finish this. This was the same deal that she offered her son-in-law and his friends and look at where it got them today.

Since she was talking about honour, she and her son-in-law would throw away all their weapons so Ms. Sophia can see that they both are unarmed

Ms. Sophia said to her that she talked as much.

Both agent Knox and Bryan threw away their weapons and Bryan immediately attacked Robert while Mrs. Harper attacked Ms. Sophia. They gave each other a hell of a beating. They fought for a few minutes before they heard the US force units announcing from outside that everyone inside should drop their weapons and come out with their hands in the air because they are coming in and if anyone tries to shoot at them first that they won't hesitate to shoot backs.

After hearing that announcement outside weakened and exhausted from the fight, Bryan, Mrs, Harper, Ms Sophia and Robert stopped fighting each other The FBI agents came in and arrested all of them.

_On the way outside, Ms. Sophia said to herself there is no way that she is going to hand herself over to the US law enforcement, for them to prosecute her for all of her crimes and atrocities, she grabs the gun off the arresting FBI agent and shot herself.

While they were taking the others outside, the FBI agent checked to see whether Ms. Sophia was still alive. They confirmed she was dead. The secret agents still loyal to Ms Sophie refused to surrender to the US forces units and shot back at them. A gun battle ensued and all the agents were killed.

Meanwhile, before they got arrested, the US navy's warship detected the incoming missile and they redirected it to the closest desert. They traced the location the missile came from and they were all shocked that it came from the CIA headquarters office. They informed the other US force units that the CIA headquarters was under attack and sent troops.

None of the CIA agents based at headquarters even realised there was an underground bunker, such was the secrecy. They didn't hear the attacks happening.

Bryan and Mrs. Harper went outside with the FBI agents that arrested them and saw Mr. Viktor and some of his men who were still alive were also arrested. The FBI agents took them all in to identify and questioned them as they did. Bryan removed the fake face he was wearing after they got to that new site, it was much easier for them to identify who he was.

They moved him into solitary confinement because the director of the FBI was still confused about what was going on. He was also confused to find Agent Knox alive because everybody knew about her death. Those FBI agents questioned everyone excluding Bryan. All had the same story, except for Robert. Robert demanded that they should remove the handcuffs they put on him and release him with immediate effect. The FBI agents interrogated him and kept on asking him what was he doing inside the new site but he kept on ordering them to release him.

The FBI agents went to their director to report to him what was going on. The FBI director said to them that this whole thing that was going on was still shocking to him because he didn't know who to believe. They should make sure that they keep an eye on Robert and make sure that he did not try to escape until they get to the bottom of this case. Why would the CIA director shoot herself if there was nothing to hide or she had no involvement in. Whatever was going on inside that new site, Robert had something to do with it.

The FBI director started to have some doubts in him that Bryan was responsible for all the crimes they accused him of. If Bryan was involved why did he hand himself over to them without a fight? If it was because we had corned him and gave him no chance to escape, then what about Mrs. Harper and the Russians?

And there was no way that the Russians will hand themselves over to US law enforcement without a fight. They should make sure that they are the ones who carried out all forensic tests and results at the crime scene. No one should inform any news broadcasting channels about the incidents so they can carry out all their forensic results without anyone trying to tamper with the evidence at that crime scene.

One of the FBI agents came in and told the FBI director that there was a man downstairs who said that he had some evidence that might help them to solve this case.

The FBI director said to the agent to send him to his office, which he did. When the FBI director looked up and saw that it was Ronald, he said to him, where the hell are you coming from?

He thought that Ronald was dead, and it seems like today was the day for dead people to return to life. First, it was agent Knox and now him.

Ronald said to him that he was going to tell him everything later but right now, the thing that was most important to him was to save his family.

The FBI director asked him if he knew that he can have him arrested right now?

Ronald said to him that he has he already knew what might happen to him the time he followed them down to the headquarters but he cared less because his family's freedom mattered a lot to him. Since he is the one that has some evidence that might set his family free, why should he sit back and watch his family go down for crimes they did not commit?

The FBI director said to him, I guess you are right because I would do the same thing for my loved ones. Let me see this evidence you have on you. I hope it will help us solves this case. If not, he would be locked up inside one of the FBI cells.

Ronald showed him the evidence, that he hacked from Ms. Sophia's cell phone. He showed the FBI director the people that Ms. Sophia was involved with and who were helping her to carry out her mission.

The FBI director asked Ronald how or where did he get all this information from?

But Ronald asked if how or where he got all this information from what matters to him right now?

The FBI director answered him by saying that he's director of the FBI and he should ask, but he guessed it doesn't matter for now how or where he got all this information from because he cannot turn a blind eye to what he just saw.

He passed down the information he got from Ronald and gave it to his investigating agents and told them that they should immediately go and arrest Mr. William, Richard and Charles and bring them all in for questioning before they find out what happened and try to flee the country. The FBI agents left and arrested Mr. William, Richard and Charles and brought them all in for questioning.

The FBI director asked Ronald whether he had more evidence because these are not ordinary men, they are in positions of power.

Ronald said to him that he can get more evidence but only if he gives him a computer so that he can hack inside Ms. Sophia's cell phone.

The FBI director said to him, enough of this hacking that he's going to get a court order allowing them to access Ms. Sophia's information freely. Even though she was dead she still has her rights.

So he requested the court order which was received, but all the messages on Ms. Sophia's cell phone were encrypted. The FBI IT agents tried to access it but they can't. Each time, it forces their computers to show blue screens and then shuts them down. So the FBI director asked Ronald to see if he can do his thing, that he's only allowing him this one time to hack the data. Ronald managed and hacked Ms. Sophia's cell phone and they got all the evidence they needed.

The forensic results came back and they matched the stories that Ms. Sophia was the one behind all those attacks with the help of Robert, Mr. William, Richard and Charles. The FBI director called the White House and direct his call to Madam President because he said that it was a matter of national security and that he needs to speak only to Madam President.

He told Madam President about what happened and Madam President ordered him to bring both Bryan, Mrs. Harper, Ronald and the Russians to the White House.

The FBI complied with the President's wishes and arranged a convoy of black SUV vehicles to take them to the White House. While they walked to the cars, US force units were there, praising and thanking them all for their bravery and for saving the world from chaos.

Bryan asked the FBI director where the convoy was going to take them.

He answered, to the White House.

Bryan said to him that he's not going anywhere with them until he finds out that his wife Juliette was safe.

The FBI director gave him his phone to call Juliette. The FBI director told Bryan to give him the location of his wife so he can personally go with some of his agents and fetch her and bring her to the White House. Bryan informed the FBI director where she was.

And they all travelled to the White House with secret service agents driving them. Before arriving at the White House, they stopped at a building where they could freshen up and change their clothes, out of the bloodstained and smoke-filled clothes they had been arrested in.

When they reached the White House, they found that the Madam President had already set up a big celebration party for them with some of her cabinet waiting for them to arrive. On entering the White House, Madam President with her cabinet members welcomed them all in and asked them all to have a seat because this party was for them. It was also her little way to thank and to apologize to them.

They all took their seats and a few minutes later, Juliette and Jason arrived with the FBI director. Madam president called for everyone's attention and told them her speech would be on lives news. She said that the celebration party this evening was for both all these brave citizens of America and for all these Russian citizens also. And she went on to say she has pardoned Bryan, and he's no longer America most wanted criminal but a free man. And she wants to say thank you to the former CIA agent, Agent Knox and the Russians, Mr. Viktor, his son and his men and finally but not the least she also wants to thank Bryan's friends and every US law enforcement unit that played a part in saving lives today.

And as for Bryan's friend George, the one that died, he is going to be buried with the full honour that befitting an American soldier. On the day of his funeral all the American flags will be drawn at half-mast to honour his death and for all the ones that died both in Britain and in Russia and the other nations where missile attacks happened.

She hereby declares that every year on this date will be a public holiday to mark the day that both American and Russian citizens united together to save the world from chaos She is hereby calling and taxing the US justice departments with one job, to make sure that they do everything in their powers so, that the people who were involved or helped in carrying out those attacks get the punishment they deserve.

After Madam President's speech, everyone applauded and everyone at the party congratulated them all for their braveness.

Juliette told Bryan they are having a baby soon. On the way to the White House she had asked the FBI director to make a quick stop at a pharmacy, where she bought some pregnancy test kits. She tested each one and they all showed positive. She showed it to Bryan and Bryan said that everything keeps getting better. He embraced and kissed his wife and thanked her for not giving up on him.

He told her that he needs to thank and share this good news with his friends, Mr. Viktor, Igor his son and his men so they all can celebrate together.

He left and Juliette saw her mother talking to Madam President. Madam President told her that she wants her back as a CIA agent and she can be the CIA director if she wants because she needs someone that she can trust.

Agent Knox said to her, that she didn't know what answers to give her right now but she wanted to take time and celebrate this moment and this night with her loved ones.

Madam President said to her that she understood where she was coming from and she should take all the time she needed but not so long because she will be waiting for her to give some feedback. She mustn't keep her president waiting too long, or was that what she was planning to do?

And agent Knox replied "no" and they both laughed. Madam President left her and Juliette was going towards her mother. She saw the way her mother was looking at Mr. Viktor and she asked her whether she liked him?

Her mother asked her who?

Juliette told her mother to stop acting like she didn't know who she was talking about.

Juliette told her mother that since she didn't know who she was talking about, she saw the way she has been looking at Mr. Viktor.

Mrs. Harper said oh! Mr. Viktor what about him?

Juliette said to her mother, I knew you liked him, I saw the way you have been admiring him even back on the island.

Mrs. Harper said to her daughter, ok you got me there. I might like him just a little bit and there was nothing wrong with tasting what the Russian man was made of. They both laughed together.

Mrs. Harper asked her whether she told Bryan about her pregnancy.

Juliette replied, yes.

Mrs. Harper asked Juliette what was his expression when she told him?

Juliette answered that he was so excited and he can't wait to share the good news with his friends.

Mrs. Harper said that she didn't know why men act the same way whenever their wives tell them that they are pregnant that they can't wait to share and celebrates the good news with all their friends like they are the ones who are going to give birth to the child.

It reminded her of the day she told her father that they were having her. She never saw her father as excited as that day. She was happy that her Juliette, her lovely beautiful daughter, also found a man who loved her and appreciated her just as her father did to her.

After their heroes' celebration party at the White House, they all went back to the island together. Bryan with his wife and his friends, while Mrs. Harper with Mr. Viktor, Igor and his men. The other CIA agents secretly took Ms. Sophia dead body and secretly buried her and also while Robert, Mr. William, Richard and Charles were sentenced to life imprisonment with hard labour.

# SUMMARY

WAS IT, WORTH IT? – Was a fantasy story to ask you leaders or you people who are using your powers, fame and influence to hide and oppose the truth from coming out - was it worth it?

No matter how long you try to oppose or hide the truth from coming out, it will surely come out one way or the other and when it does come out, all the people that you have been intimidating with your powers or have been hiding the truth from will eventually turn and fight against you

Look at what happened to Ms. Sophia and her team members when the people they had been abusing and lying to, find out about the truth – they came back to fight them. Ms. Sophia thought just because she was now the CIA director that she was untouchable, that she can use her influence to treat and use anyone the ways she wanted and they wouldn't find out about the truth. Despite this, they do find out about the truth and they can't do anything to her because she has some ways of burying the truth. But for how long was she going to hide the truth away? She was forgetting that the same way she climbed the ladder and got her way to the top was the same way that she was going to fall. When the truth does come out and Bryan finds out that she was using him to climb to the top of the ladder. With the help of his mother-in-law, Mr. Viktor, his men and his friends all teaming up with the help of US law enforcement to fight against them, she ends up shooting herself and leaving her team members behind to face the law, because she can't stand to face the truth.

It also asks, if Ms. Sophia and all her team members that all these lies, deceit and other horrible things they did to the innocent people and the innocent lives they sacrificed for them to climb to the top of their ladders - was it worth it?

It's also up to you whether you have been afraid of saying the truth or standing up for what is right because of the fears of what might happen to you - was it worth it?

The truth that you have or know about might set an innocent victim or victims free, but just because you are fearful of what the person or the people that might be exposed in the process might do to you, you choose to mind your own business and sit back and watch while an innocent victim or victims takes the falls. Take Ronald as an example; even though he already knows what might happen to him, he chose not to talk about it because he has something that might set his loved ones free. Even if you are afraid of what might happen to you when they find out that it was you who gave the evidence that exposed them, why not send it in as anonymous so that justice will be served.

It also to ask you that if you don't always have time for your loved ones - was it worth it? Because you don't have to wait until you lose your loved ones before you then realise family is more important than any other thing in this world. Look at Mr. Viktor and how long it took him to realise his son Igor was the only thing that mattered to him. When he came to America with his son, Igor, he thought that his arms and nuclear weapons business back in Russia was the thing that mattered most to him until he lost his son Igor. He then realised that his son was the only thing that mattered to him. When he finds out the truth, the same people that he moved to America for were the same people that he begged to the point that he agreed to share half of all his assets with them so they can help him avenge his son's death.

It is also to ask both the American and Russian nations that all these things that you are buying and developing to prove that you are superior to the other – for example nuclear bombs, missiles, ammunitions etc. was it worth it? Instead, you two nations could put your difference aside and unite together just as Mrs. Harper and Mr. Viktor did to save the world from chaos. Both nations will unite together by putting their difference aside and fighting real wars that are going on, in the world, for example, starvation, racism, poverty etc.

It is also to ask the world leaders some questions. All these false and empties promises that they make to their citizens through the time of the elections - was it worth it? They all know full well that once they are elected into an office that they won't enact even half of what they have promised the citizens during their political campaigns. Once they are elected, they will look after their own and their political party's interests. Looking at Mr. William for example with his position in life, why did he have to join Ms. Sophia's team? He has already had the money, power, fame and assets that some people pray and wish they might have just a quarter of what he had, but Mr. William wants more. So, to the world leaders no matter what you have, you will still want more because that's the nature of being a human being so try to include the interests of your nation's citizens in both your own self-interests and political party's agendas.

It also to ask the world leaders that all this money you all have been paid every year - was it worth it? Because you all spend a large proportion of your nations yearly budgets on buying and developing nuclear weapons, missiles, ammunitions etc. and preparing for World War III. No one knows where it is going to happen and when this war starts it is the citizens who have already been dying and suffering from poverty that are going to suffer during this war. So instead of them spending so much money every year on all those weapons, why don't they spend some of that money in tackling the ongoing poverty that has been happening in their own nations.

It is also asking the world leaders about all these wars that they have been sending their soldiers into - was it worth it? Because you all always seem to ignore or act like you don't know the damage all those wars have caused to your soldier's mental health. And you treat those soldiers after coming back from wars like they are nothing. By allowing them to retire and live among your nation's citizens with the traumas from those wars that have damaged their mental health which might lead them to be toxic towards the people around them.

Looking at the damage it caused to George's mental health that lead him to start using substances to calm himself down. And also to Bryan, it led him to fight the system. Instead of allowing those soldiers to retire and live among other citizens why not allow those soldiers to live in army camps and find them other jobs that they might be doing whilst in the army. After coming back from those wars, they should attend some therapy sessions for their own well-being and for their mental health.

It also to ask the world that all this hatred placed towards women and the LGBT societies when it comes to being involved in a nation's leadership – was it worth it? Because the world knows what might happen if they are given a chance to be part of the government or leading the nation. Looking at Madam President's leadership, for example, the works that she did, even when there was a time that Ms. Sophia tried to trick her into making Bryan the world's number one enemy, she refused and stood up for what she knew was the truth. She also understood that her job was to protect all her citizens. Maybe by giving women and the LGBT societies chances to be part of the nation's leadership, they are the ones that might bring positive changes that the world has been looking for.

I THANK YOU!!!

## ABOUT THE AUTHOR

ONYEKA-NWAEME was born on 1st July 1994 and he moved to South Africa in 2016.
After his first non -fiction title "TEARS AND JOY OF NAYOMI" was published, he fell in love with writing books and being an author.

www.ingramcontent.com/pod-product-compliance
Lightning Source LLC
Chambersburg PA
CBHW030232180626
46810CB00008B/3085